DARK DESTINY

THIEF OF HEARTS

C.R. JANE

MILA YOUNG

CONTENTS

Dark Destiny by C. R. Jane and Mila Young

Copyright © 2020 by C. R. Jane and Mila Young

All rights reserved.

No portion of this book may be reproduced in any form or by any electronic or mechanical means, including information storage and retrieval systems, without written permission from the author, except for the use of brief quotations in a book review, and except as permitted by U.S. copyright law.

For permissions contact:

crjaneauthor@gmail.com

milayoungarc@gmail.com

This book is a work of fiction. Names, characters, businesses, places, events, locales, and incidents are either the products of the author's imagination or used in a fictitious manner. Any resemblance to actual persons, living or dead, or actual events is purely coincidental.

To all the readers who can't choose.

DARK DESTINY

The sirens have been captives for so long that we no longer remember our pasts...

Our masters have stolen our song, the source of all our power, and made it punishable by death to use it. Our bodies, our minds, and our talents all belong to them.

The vampires.

I've been sent to the darkest of all places, Nightmare Penitentiary for my next assignment. But I've promised myself this assignment will be my last... no matter the cost. I'll do whatever it takes to free my people, even if I end up shattering the hearts of three captivating men who have the power to change my future forever.

One will sacrifice himself for me. One will shatter my soul. And one will kill me to save me.

Welcome to Nightmare Penitentiary. Escape is my only option.

CHAPTER 1

It was midnight.

My birthday.

And wasn't it ironic that today was both the beginning and the end of my life?

Or at least, that was what it felt like.

Because you see, today, my powers were going to finally come to me.

And today, the vampires would take it.

* * *

I sat on my bed, fiddling with the gossamer threads. Anyone who looked at my life from the outside would think that I'm privileged, spoiled even. But they don't know anything about me.

I stretched out, blowing out a sigh as I waited for

my powers to come in. It was past midnight. Had they come in already? Was I supposed to feel something?

I was kind of expecting something cool to happen. Maybe a burst of light, a chorus of angels...something.

So far, none of that had happened.

I opened my mouth and sang a verse of my favorite Halsey song because humans really know their music...but nothing feels different.

And so, I wait.

A lot of the other girls I talked to didn't really know what it felt like to use their power, and they refused to talk about what it felt like to receive the power at all. They reasoned that because they were going to lose it anyway, what was the point of using it at all? That way, they would never know what they were missing.

But I couldn't do that.

I had to know just for a few seconds if that's all I got, what it felt like to be powerful. To be whole. To be what I was born to be.

The vampires made sure the rest of our lives never felt like that.

My mind inevitably drifted to tomorrow, and what that meant for me.

Tomorrow, I would enter the family business. Mama had been grooming me for it for the last few years. How to dress...how to talk...how to act...how to please a man. How to be a beautiful face and nothing else.

A lifetime of being nothing. That's what eighteen meant for me.

I once read a book about the sirens. I found it in the school library, and although I'm sure that most of it wasn't true, one thing did stand out to me.

Sirens once had control. The waves, the depths of the sea, the weather...all of it was ours.

And then one day, all that power disappeared.

My thoughts dissipated as my chest started to burn. I rubbed it absentmindedly, thinking maybe I had some indigestion from all that lettuce my mother had forced me to eat for dinner.

The burning began to spread, however, until I felt like I was on fire. Looking down at my skin in panic, I half expected it to look burnt to a crisp.

The pain grew so intense that I opened my mouth to scream, but nothing came out. It was like I was being reborn at that moment, changed from the inside out.

I laid there and felt like I was dying as the burning somehow intensified until my world was narrowed to just a pinprick in space. No wonder none of the girls I knew had wanted to talk about this. I couldn't imagine a greater pain than this. I guess this explained how my mama could do unmedicated childbirth like it was nothing.

Just when I thought I couldn't take a second more, and the burning became so great that I believed I would become nothing but embers at any time, the burning disappeared as quickly as it had begun. It left me a throbbing, shaking mess from the adrenaline still coursing through my body.

Tears were streaming down my face. I had been in so much pain that I didn't even realize that I was crying.

Lifting my hand to brush the tears off my face, I gasped in surprise. The skin on my hand almost seemed to be glowing...it was like there was a backlight reflecting off my hand. I started examining my entire body and saw that the strange light had taken over every inch of my skin. There were other changes as well.

I was more…

That was the best way to describe it. My skin was smoother, my dark hair was thicker and longer, my lips were fuller...everything about my looks was just...more.

What was even stranger than the way my skin glowed and what also seemed to have improved, was the fact that I felt stronger. Like there was a power inside of me that was just waiting to come out and play.

And I didn't even have to wonder what it was. I just knew. It hummed through my mind.

I opened my mouth, and it was just instinct, this song that I was all of a sudden singing. A song as old as time itself. A song of my people.

It flowed from me, weaving its spell on everything around me. Storm clouds were gathering in the distance outside the window I now stood in front of.

Wind was picking up from the east and racing towards me. All of nature was bending to my will.

I felt powerful. I felt magical. I felt like who I was supposed to be.

I didn't know how I could live without this feeling ever again.

* * *

I woke up in a daze. At first, I didn't realize where I was. The last thing I remembered was standing in the pouring rain in my manor's back-yard as the wind raced around me.

Somehow, I ended up back in my room on the floor.

And somehow, I fell asleep.

Staring at the clock, I wanted to cry. Julian would be here any minute. And then everything would be gone.

A knock sounded on my door just then, and a hiccupping sob burst out of my mouth.

The door opened a second later, and Mama stood there, perfectly primped and coiffed as ever. She was Julian's little pet.

And I hated her for it.

I hated her acceptance of our life. I hated that she'd paraded me in front of Julian since I was a little girl, and that she ignored the heated glances he gave me.

She ignored the promise in his eyes for what was to come for me.

She was a selfish, terrible excuse for a woman. If only her outside appearance matched the ugliness inside of her.

She looked triumphant as she stared at me from the doorway.

Rosalind Alexander was a beautiful woman. And beautiful was probably an understatement. She was stunning. The kind of being who garnered stares no matter where she was or who she was talking to.

She was the darling of the vampires' courtesans, and very proud of that fact. Icy blonde hair, blue eyes that could and did charm any man. She was perfect, perfectly evil.

"What are you doing on the floor?" she asked disdainfully.

As much as I wanted to tell her to go fuck herself, I refrained.

"Julian will be here soon. Get changed," she ordered, looking at my pajamas that consisted of an old rock concert tee and a pair of cheerleading shorts like they were disease-ridden.

"Yes ma'am," I replied, trying my best to sound respectful. Because she controlled my future right now. I was hopeful that at the very least, she would ease me into the business rather than throwing me to the wolves all at once.

When I didn't move quick enough for her liking,

she marched over to me and slapped me on the side of my head. "Get up," she barked before striding away, confident that her orders would be obeyed. She'd specifically hit me on the side of my head rather than my face so that there wouldn't be any visible blemishes. Julian wouldn't like that, and all my mama cared about was him.

Wasn't it a pity for her that all she wanted in life was him and all he wanted was me?

I shivered at the thought.

I went through the motions of getting ready. There was a certain order to getting ready that I'd been taught practically before I could walk.

Wash my face, moisturize my face, apply lotion all over my body. Apply makeup. Get dressed. Do my hair. Apply perfume in certain places.

I didn't even have to think about it.

Thirty minutes later, I stood there in front of my mirror, the perfect daughter once again. There were no band tees worn during the day. Just like there would be no birthday cake today. It was just how things were.

I walked over to the window, trying to delay the inevitable.

I could still feel the power coursing through me. So much power that I could leave right now if I wanted to and everything would bow to me.

Except for the vampires. They would eventually find me. And then they would destroy me. Just as they had any siren who dared to step out of line in the past.

We didn't talk about it, but my great-grandmother had been one of those killed for daring to rebel. It was my family's greatest shame, one my mother and grandmother spent their whole lives rectifying. It was only me that secretly thought about her. Thought about her and wanted to be like her.

Without the whole dying part though obviously.

I wasn't sure how the vampires did it. But it was a principle in the paranormal world that everything had something that was bigger and badder than them. And although the sirens were much more powerful than many of the paranormal creatures out there, the simplest explanation was that the vampire was the siren's shark. Ten out of ten times, the shark would beat the fish. And ten out of ten times, the vampire crushed the sirens.

Another knock sounded on the door, and I wanted to cry. I opened my window and quickly began to gather storm clouds, the process instinctive. As the perfectly sunny day suddenly became dark and cloudy, and rain began to fall, I savored the mist coming in through the window, even though it was ruining my hair. I would take my punishment for not looking perfect, just so I could feel it one last time.

The knock beat on the door again, this time louder and more urgent.

"Coming," I called out sharply, even knowing that the servant on the other side of the door was just doing their job and had no role in this.

I took one last inhale, memorizing the way I felt at this moment, and then I closed the window and walked to the door, not bothering to fix my appearance one bit.

Betsy, one of our maids, was waiting for me outside the door. She was usually one of my favorite servants, always full of gossip and intrigue to tell me. But today I couldn't even muster up a smile for her.

"Happy Birthday, miss," she said softly, and I nodded at her in acknowledgment, proud of myself for managing to keep my lip from quivering.

She examined me as we walked, and I knew she was noting how different I looked at the moment. I knew most of the changes would disappear after Julian did whatever he was going to do. The glow in my skin would definitely go. But there were some things that would stay, like my longer hair and eyelashes and my larger lips. Traits I wasn't grateful for in the least bit. I had enough time trying to keep beings away from me, I didn't need even more things enticing them.

Betsy didn't understand, but the reason she liked me so much, the reason why she had no problem working hard for us around the house day after day for practically nothing wasn't because of my naturally winsome personality. No, instead it was because all sirens were born with something that attracted everyone around them. Some sirens were more powerful than others, but we all held that same basic trait. Men...and women...happened to fall in love with us, wanted to be our friend, wanted to be near us, all the time. It wasn't something that could be taken away. It was just intrinsic to our very nature. Of course, that whole shark thing came into play with that ability as well, and the vampires didn't have a problem falling in love with us. Instead, they used our ability to get what they wanted from other species, and they used our above-average looks to give themselves pleasure.

The Goddess Mother up in the heavens must have had a cruel sense of humor.

"You look nice, miss," Betsy commented softly and it was all I could do not to roll my eyes. I controlled myself, even though the looks of pity and lust she was throwing my way made me want to punch her in her friendly face.

We finally made it into the "parlor" as Mama called it, which really was just a glorified term for living room.

And there he was.

Julian Morgenstern in all of his glory.

And he really was a glorious sight. The perfect predator to drag in his prey. His eyes immediately met mine as I entered the room, and his mouth curled up into a possessive smile.

Although I knew Julian was at least a few thousand years old, he would appear to any human to be in his mid-30s. He had blonde hair that was almost silver looking, it was so light. His hair was offset by his striking dark brown eyes, so dark that they almost appeared black if you weren't in good lighting. He was tall, with perfectly carved muscles that, thanks to his vampire heritage, would always be there...even if he decided to eat bonbons on the couch for the rest of his life. He had an aristocratic nose and a cruel mouth, and everything about him made me want to flee his presence.

Women of all species fell all over themselves to be with him, but for reasons unknown to me, all Julian Morgenstern wanted was me.

His eyes greedily took me in, not missing a detail. He didn't seem perturbed at all by the fact that my hair was wet from the storm I'd created. If anything, he looked excited about it.

"She's strong, Rosalind," he commented, beginning to walk a slow circle around me as he examined me from all angles. "Much stronger than I thought. It's almost a shame..."

I stiffened, hoping against all odds that he was actually thinking about letting me keep my power.

It was a stupid hope though. Julian suddenly called for his servant, Frederick, to bring him something.

I thought about getting on my knees to beg, or calling for a storm, or running like I dreamed about earlier. But I did none of that. I just stood there like my feet had turned into stone.

Frederick walked over to him and handed him an object covered in a silky red cloth. Julian carefully pulled off the cloth, revealing what looked like some kind of glass ball.

"Look familiar, Rosalind?" Julian commented when he noticed how Mama's eyes were locked onto the ball.

I glanced at her, confused. But I didn't stay confused long.

Julian walked towards me until he was standing uncomfortably close to me. He stared down at me feverishly for a moment.

What happened next would live in my dreams for a very long time. Julian opened his mouth, so wide that his jaw looked like it had become dislocated. I stared into the black hole of his mouth, terrified as he began to make a strange sucking sound.

As soon as the sound began, I experienced a strange pulling sensation. As if my life source was being siphoned out of me. I tried to move as a gold mist began to stream out of me, but I was locked into place. All I could do was watch horrified as the gold mist— which I recognized to be my power, based on how weak I was beginning to feel—floated into the glass orb.

Julian's eyes rolled backwards in pleasure.

He had always been the baddest monster in the room...but this was on a whole other level.

Julian took every last drop of my power.

And when he was done, and the glass orb was pulsing with the golden light of what he had stolen from me...I felt like I had died.

CHAPTER 2

*L*oathing.

That was all I felt. Utter loathing.

"You look beautiful tonight, Selena," Julian whispered in my ear, his heavy breath washing across my cheek before pulling back.

I stood deadly still, knowing where the conversation was headed. I'd expected it, but I'd hoped it wouldn't come just yet. Not at my birthday party. And not after what he'd done to me just this morning.

Of course, Julian wasn't about to lose out on what he thought was his. He was here to claim his property.

Me.

I hate you, I wanted to say. *I hate you so much that I'd die before I let you touch me.*

"I'm nothing like my mother when it comes to beauty," I commented dryly, noting that Mama was watching us aptly, something like jealousy flaring in her fathomless eyes.

Something in his dark gaze shifted, a warning that I stepped too close to the truth. He bedded her from time to time, but his eyes always lingered on me when he'd visit our home, looking at me with something deplorable in his gaze. It always left me feeling filthy.

"You know you've always been my special girl." The slimy ass's eyes dipped to my mouth, then my chest. My skin crawled, and I suddenly regretted wearing the strapless chiffon dress. The back of his knuckles traced down my cheek, and I winced.

Julian stared straight into my eyes, the tips of his fangs slipping over the top of his lower lip. A show of power, of dominance. The room spun, but I blinked past the dizziness.

It was funny the things that went through your mind when facing a monster, when you were in pain and trying to look brave. The music changed to a slow ballad, a song I'd loved for so long. It told the tale of a girl who lost her true love to death. How they'd been born with a string between their hearts that declared their destiny to be together, but it had snapped when he died. The similarities to her life and mine struck a cord. She'd tragically lost her man, while I'd lost part of my soul to this vampire. I was sure my body would be next.

Fury flared through me at just the idea of it. My body was still exhausted from this morning's event. It was like I was never going to feel the same again, even though I'd only had a few hours with my powers.

"You know… we could make a deal," he said, tracing the skin across my collarbone as his tongue peeked out to wet his bottom lip.

I did my best to hide my revulsion at his touch. Julian considered himself a businessman, but in reality, he was nothing but a glorified pimp. It was too bad that siren trafficking was such a lucrative industry. With all the money he made, he was able to run Chicago.

I twisted my lips into a smile to avoid making a scene, just as Mama had taught me. *Never shed a tear,* she'd say. *A lady never shows her emotions.*

I'd never been able to wear the same blank mask that she wore.

"I'm not really much of a businesswoman," I finally responded, and his dark eyes flared from my impunity.

Mama's voice grew louder from somewhere in the background just then. Seemingly louder than the chatter of a room with more than a hundred people. Did she turn a blind eye, knowing too well that Julian had planned to claim me this whole time?

I scrunched up my toes in my stilettos.

"Tomorrow," he muttered, his voice low and dark. "I'm coming for you. You will give me everything." His gaze dropped down and back up my body once more, making his intentions clear.

Unsavory words bubbled on the forefront of my mind. Mostly consisting of curses, and I yearned to unleash them. To tell him to go fuck himself. And this time, I couldn't stop myself.

"I'd rather rot in hell," I hissed through clenched teeth.

"You'd better change your attitude quickly, Selena. I'm not a patient man." He reached over and grasped my chin between his thumb and index finger, forcing my head high to stare at him.

Fear rippled up my spine at the possessive darkness I saw swirling in his gaze.

Control your emotions. Just as I'd been taught my whole life. This was why I'd been taught that lesson. There was no out for me in this situation.

Bile rose up my throat, and the salad I'd eaten earlier threatened to come out.

The easy path was to be like the rest of the sirens. The consequences of not following the rules sat heavy on my chest. I could listen to orders, do Julian's bidding, and spread my legs for him.

An ache flared in my chest at the thought. That was exactly what this asshole in front of me wanted. To be my first.

"Sir." One of Julian's henchmen appeared at his back just then. A tall man with a shaved head, dressed in a tailored suit. Pure muscle but my savior at that moment.

Julian let out an indistinguishable grunt, released me, and turned around with a serious glare.

I used that moment to slip out from under his

attention and quickly rushed away. I didn't recognize most of the attendees at my party. Distinguished families. Siren and vampire alike. None of my friends from school had been invited of course. Mama didn't even know I had friends at school.

In truth, this celebration wasn't really a party for me, but a declaration that I'd reached an age to enter the business.

Out into the hallway, I pushed into the ladies' room before locking the door behind me. Mirrors lined one side of the wall with white leather seats in front of them. More chandeliers decorated the room. Another door led to the toilets.

I pressed my back to the wall, my body shaking. I wasn't ready to be owned. To give my body away night after night at someone's bidding. I craved so much more out of life… most of all, I yearned for freedom.

Tears slid out of the corners of my eyes, and I wiped them away.

Glancing up at the full-length mirror in front of me, I stared at a girl I didn't recognize. My face full of make-up, my bare shoulders glistened with glitter, my dress as blue as the brightest ocean. Dark hair fell down in soft waves over my shoulders, the tips dipped in blue. Eyes just as blue. My dress cinched around my body. Earlier, I loved how the gown followed my small curves. But now, I wanted to tear it off me, hating the way it enticed Julian to leer at me.

I looked lost.

I wanted to be lost.

I felt more desperation at that moment than I'd ever felt before.

It's your job to look captivating, Mama had said. *With just enough skin to tempt them, but not enough to drive them to insanity.*

I bit my tongue until it hurt, until I felt nothing but sharpness. Until I tasted the coppery flood of blood in my mouth.

For so long, I tried to hold onto some semblance of control over my life. Going to school, having friends, attending parties. Normal things. But I'd been trying to live a life that could never be mine.

I was made up of broken pieces. And instead of finding a way to put myself back together, I was about to be shattered into a dozen more.

Tap, tap, tap.

A knock sounded on the door, insistent, and panic spiked through me.

It couldn't be him, he couldn't touch me tonight. Not yet. I moved to the door and with a flick, unlocked it, then opened it.

A woman with a skin-tight violet dress sighed. "About time." She rolled her eyes at me and shoved inside past me.

My stomach fell with relief that it wasn't Julian. I stepped outside into the hallway. People were mingling everywhere until Mama emerged from the ballroom, searching the area.

Hell, I was in trouble.

When she spotted me, her back straightened, then she marched over to me. Her perfect white gown shimmered beneath the chandeliers, the long fabric swishing left and right with her fast steps. She was the epitome of perfection.

And the thing was… I didn't want to be perfect like her. I had learned early on that the ugliest things were inside the prettiest of faces.

"Why are you hiding out here?" She grabbed my arm and squeezed hard.

"I just… I needed some air."

"Selena, this is your birthday party. You need to be in there, entertaining our guests."

"I hardly know anyone here. These aren't my friends."

Mama's scowl deepened, her fingernails digging into my arms. "Do not embarrass yourself or our family any more than you already have." She leaned closer, looked around to ensure we were alone, and whispered, "Do you think I didn't see that you pissed Julian off earlier? He paid for the whole event. Trust me, you don't want to see his dark side. Just follow the rules," she hissed.

Rules. Right.

Except, I fucking hated rules.

"You have five seconds to march back in there." Her eyes were fuming, and if we weren't at this party, I'd be feeling the palm of her hand right now against my face.

Gritting my teeth, I lifted my chin before waltzing back toward the ballroom, leaving Mama behind. I could do this. Just a few painstakingly awful hours pretending to be happy.

Pretending I was the perfect daughter.

Pretending I lived in a perfect home.

Pretending I couldn't wait to accept my role.

All perfect little lies.

I was going to make sure tonight that I wouldn't ever be considered perfect again.

CHAPTER 3

The wind violently ripped through my hair. I was running down the sidewalk, night cloaking the city. The party ended a couple of hours ago, and as soon as we arrived home, I feigned exhaustion and went to my room. Then, I snuck out.

A quick glance behind me, Mama or Julian hadn't seen me leave. There were no shadows stalking me through the night. The family mansion sat at the end of the street like an overbearing mountain, cloaked in the dark. With only one light on shining through the night… Mama's bedroom. The two-story house had started to feel more like a prison with each passing day. After tonight, I wasn't sure what would become of me, or even where I'd end up living. Many of the girls working for Julian moved into specific homes where they were watched 24/7. I shuddered at the thought of him moving me into his private residence.

I was determined that wasn't going to be an attractive option for him after tonight.

On my last night of freedom, I chose to get away from everyone. At the corner of the street, I flagged a passing cab and climbed into the back.

"The farthest bar across town as you can find."

"Yes, miss." He began to drive, giving me a long glance through the rear view mirror as all guys did. "You look a little young to be going to a bar," he commented like he was concerned, but I could see the hunger in his gaze. He was staring at me so much, I was a little afraid we were going to drive off the road.

"People always say that," I commented dryly.

I had no plans on following rules like age restrictions tonight.

"It's my birthday today," I murmured, more to myself. And that meant going as far as possible with the help of a little alcohol

"Happy birthday. Get anything special?"

I lifted my gaze to the soft gray eyes looking at me from the mirror.

I don't know if I would call today "special."

I blinked at him, then looked away, staring at the houses that blurred as we passed them. "Not really."

Special. I wanted to laugh at just the idea of how today could have gone if I was anything else but what I was.

How did our kind fall so far? What had it been like before?

Half an hour later, and we finally pulled up in front of a bar. "The farthest bar and least seediest for a pretty lady."

I stared outside the window. Black walls and glass doors. Inside, people were everywhere, the music thumping and reaching me in the back of the cab. It was dimly lit. It was perfect. I'd be a nobody and drown every sorrow I had in a glass of something strong until I forgot everything.

I handed the driver a fifty-dollar bill. "Thank you." I climbed out, not bothering with change and patted down my black skin-tight dress. Of course, I'd changed clothes into something more me before leaving the house.

A black, A-line scoop neck dress, cascading half way down to my thighs. Julian had once seen me wearing this dress and threatened me with bodily harm if anyone ever saw me in it but him. I loved the dress even more after that.

The bouncer to the bar eyed my approach, scrutinizing me.

"ID, please," he said without hesitation.

"Why would you possibly need that?" I replied in a voice that came out almost musical, and a surge of energy flared over my skin. I met his gaze and fluttered my eyes, placing a hand on his strong bicep. "You can see that I'm old enough."

A stupid grin spread over his face, the stoic expression chased away by something I couldn't quite put my finger on. Admiration. No. It was more than that. It was devotion. He stared at me as if he'd do anything I asked at that moment. And all it took was a few words, a touch. It surprised me how quickly he grew obedient.

"Where did you come from, sunshine?"

Someone really had to work on their pick up lines. "Will you let me inside the bar, please?" With my words came the flow of energy in the air between us.

He nodded and quickly opened the door. "Of course."

What the hell had just happened? I had done it without even thinking. Had some of my power survived? That wasn't supposed to happen, I was confident of that. The small taste of power almost made me sad though, it was so minuscule compared to what I'd experienced just this morning.

I strolled into the bar, feeling the bouncer's eyes on my back. I worked my way around the crowded place, on the hunt for a copious amount of alcohol to help me forget who I was. I eventually made my way to the bar.

The red-headed bartender immediately came to help me despite the fact that there were at least twenty people standing at the bar before me.

"Redbull and vodka, please," I told him calmly, and he immediately went to make my drink.

"I haven't seen you in here before," he murmured with an alluring smile that I was sure worked well on his customers, but had no effect on me.

I just smiled at him, hoping he would get the hint

that I had no interest.

He handed me a drink finally with a face that looked like I'd just kicked his puppy. When I still didn't say anything, he finally moved away to help his other customers, keeping one eye on me the whole time.

Humans. They were all the same. Although our ability to attract worked on every creature but the vampires as far as I knew, humans were particularly attracted to the energy we gave off. That bartender would be thinking of me for weeks if not years after tonight, which was really too bad for him.

"Hey, gorgeous. Are you free tonight?" a voice asked from next to me, and I looked over with a sigh. There was an older man next to me who was dressed as though he'd just stepped away from the office. He settled onto the stool next to me, his eyes devouring my form.

"No thanks," I replied calmly as I took another sip from my drink and intentionally turned the other way from him.

And that was when I saw him.

He was the most breathtaking man I've ever laid eyes on, even putting Julian's cold beauty to shame.

I'd caught his eyes, and I refused to look away. His dark chestnut hair was slicked back off his face. Strong features called to me, his square face, striking cheek-bones, and piercing green eyes crowned by thick brows. He looked maybe twenty-four or twenty-five. His arms were powerful and tanned under his midnight blue button-up shirt, the sleeves rolled up to his elbows. His broad chest filled out that top perfectly.

That half-smile slipping over his lips had my heart racing.

He was beautiful, but that was not all that hooked my attention. There was something different about him, an energy that I'd never sensed before. He was a paranormal of some kind, that much was obvious just based on his otherworldly looks alone. But I couldn't place what kind. He wasn't fae, not vampire either-thank goodness. He wasn't...anything that I'd ever sensed before. And that should've made me very wary of him, but it didn't.

I felt his eyes on me, staring, studying me. Shaking off the instinct to look away, I nibbled on the corner of my mouth. I'd never met anyone that affected me this quickly before. Who caused the eruption of butterflies in my gut, their wings beating frantically. When I met his gaze, I trembled. He, on the other hand, offered me a full smile.

At that moment, he was the solution to all my problems. This gorgeous creature was going to make me forget and give me the taste of freedom that I was desperate for. Consequences be damned.

"Listen, baby..." the annoying man on the other side of me continued, and I rolled my eyes before turning to look at him.

"I'm not interested," I scolded him coldly.

He didn't seem to get the message. "Seems like you

could use some company," he persisted as he shot me a wide grin.

I was just about to tell him off, when a smooth voice —one that sent goosebumps across my skin—spoke from behind me.

"Actually, she's here with me," he interrupted, so close to me that I could feel the whisper of his breath against my neck.

A shiver of desire traveled from the base of my spine all the way up, leaving me heated. Who was this man to affect me in such a way?

The creep in front of me groaned under his breath, his displeasure clear on his face as he stood and stalked away.

Swiveling on my stool, I came face to face with those gorgeous deep green eyes that reminded me of storm clouds bruising the sky. Sitting next to me, he turned to me, his full lips quirked into an infectious smirk. A hint of stubble graced his jaw. Legs wide, he leaned an elbow onto the bar. He seemed to blend so perfectly into the surroundings, not drawing any eyes...almost as if no one else could see him. Which was strange, considering he was the most handsome guy in the room, someone who would stand out in any crowd.

He also seemed perfectly calm.

While me... I sweated with nerves and had to wipe my wet palms down my dress.

"Some people don't understand the word 'no,'" he

said, his voice a deliciously deep baritone that practically melted me in my seat.

It took me a while to respond as I hadn't realized I sat there frozen, drowning in his presence. I was meant to hypnotize him, not the other way around. "Thanks for coming to my rescue," I said, finally finding my words.

I batted my eyes, unable to control my reaction to this man. The fire in my chest felt primal and raw. It should be me having him at my beck and call, not the other way around.

There was something dark about him, something dangerously sexy. The warning in my head pushed forward. Except, I came here for one night to get away. To escape. To find the right man to help me forget the shitshow my life was about to turn into.

And this man was exactly what I was looking for.

"I'm Katrina," I said, and reached over, placing a quick hand on his knee as I gave him the fake name I'd chosen for the night.

He glanced down at my touch then back up at me. "Keon. It means king of the kings apparently." He chuckled, the sound like a tickle on my ears.

"Really. So, you're from royalty?" I teased.

His hand slid over the top of mine, the heat from his touch zipped up my arm and flooded me instantaneously. Leaning closer, he whispered, "In a way." That devilish grin returned, and I saw in those eyes of his my earlier confirmation that he wasn't a human. Something else stirred inside him, but asking was out of the question. I wouldn't out myself if he hadn't sensed anything out of the ordinary with me yet.

Questions rippled over my mind, my upbringing pushing me to ask him about his life, his heritage, what exactly he was...anything be polite.

But I didn't actually want to know any of those things. The less I knew, the better. He was my knight in shining armor for one night. Beyond that, I wouldn't torture myself with any other details.

"What can I get you to drink?" he asked.

"I already have a drink," I told him, before realizing that I'd already drained my drink dry.

"I don't think I'm thirsty anymore," I murmured as I leaned closer to him.

"Didn't you just get here?" he responded.

I shrugged, struggling to concentrate as he put his hand on mine. The way he so easily claimed my touch and held me there in place affected me.

"I came for something else," I whispered, my cheeks flushing with heat, but I held onto his gaze. This was my night to let loose, to be anyone but myself. Julian might be claiming me tomorrow, but there was something he wouldn't be able to own tomorrow that I was going to hopefully give away to this stranger tonight.

I might never get this chance at freedom again.

The look on Keon's handsome face softened. He leaned in closer, his mouth grazing over my cheek as he reached my ear. "I promise not to hurt you."

His words left me breathless. There was no shock on his part. Did girls pick him up all the time? I wouldn't be surprised, but I didn't want to think about that today. None of that mattered.

Not when I was transfixed on his perfect lips that I wanted ravishing me. My breaths came fast and shallow. Everything about him made my body crave him, so I pushed myself off the stool. Bravery had me lifting my chin in his direction. Darkness flooded around him, people were everywhere, and the music picked up. But all I saw was this man. This stranger who captivated me.

He glanced at me, and we were at eye level. I couldn't help but notice his large hands on my hips. Fire engulfed me. He drew me closer to him, and I stumbled to stand between his strong thighs.

Exhilaration thrummed through me.

His grip slid around my lower back. We stood chest to chest, plastered to each other. Our mouths inches away, his breath warm. All I could smell was him… Intoxicating, masculine, and woodsy.

"You may be tiny, but you have a fierceness about you that is incredibly beautiful," he breathed.

I wanted to laugh out loud, because I felt anything but fierce. I was scared and desperate and controlling the only thing I had left under my power.

From the corner of my eyes, people were mingling, stealing glances my way, their eyes still seeming to flick over him.

When I turned back around, his mouth grazed mine, and he kissed me. I pressed myself closer to him, my hands splayed over his rock hard chest, and kissed him back. He plunged his tongue against the seam of my lips. I parted my lips and let him into my mouth, our tongues tangling. Shivers of excitement ran over my flesh, and a moan spilled from me.

My whole body lit up from the most incredible kiss I'd ever received. I floated on air, forgetting where I was… all I knew was that this gorgeous man was kissing me with a delicious hunger.

When he broke our kiss, I couldn't stop smiling. "That was amazing."

I felt stupid as soon as the words came out, but he didn't seem to notice. He climbed to his feet, collecting my hand in his. "Come with me."

I followed him through the crowds. Men I passed all glanced our way, hatred tossed at Keon, who they appeared to see just fine now. Jealousy radiated from the guys' gazes. Keon didn't notice. His hand around mine tightened as he rushed us to the rear of the bar. He palmed open the door and drew me into a stairwell. We were surrounded by nothing but white walls and a hum of noise from back in the bar. Before we even reached the steps, he wrenched me toward him.

I gasped as he pinned me to the wall, then turned me around to face away from him. My cheek pressed into the cold stone wall, my hands splayed on either side of me.

His chest pushed flush against my back, the hard bulge in his pants grinding up against me. His hands bunched up my skirt and found the bare cheeks of my ass. His hands were rough and confident.

My pulse thundered through my veins.

His breath grazed my ear. "Is this what you want?"

I gasped for air, my whole body burning up.

"Feeling indecisive?" he persisted, then hooked his thumbs into the elastic of my thong. I was vaguely aware of him pulling away from me and sliding my underwear down to my ankles.

"Step out of them, gorgeous," he ordered, and I obliged, melting under his dominance.

I turned to see him stuffing my bunched up thong into his pocket. He was pressed up behind me, a strong arm looped around my waist, his mouth on my neck. "Fuck, you're driving me crazy."

With a hand, he forced me back around before gripping my hips. With his strong palm sliding to my back, he pushed me to bend forward, my ass in the air, the cool breeze caressing my exposed rear. With a foot, he nudged my ankles wider apart. "Spread your legs."

My heart pounded so hard, my knees wobbled. We were going to do it here, like this? I hadn't given this a complete think through or had any expectations. But did it matter? I wanted one thing from him, and he was about to deliver.

The rational part of my mind insisted I should suggest a different location, with me facing him. But there was nothing rational about tonight. Instead, a sharp edge of desire rippled through me, and I held back the moan pressing on my throat.

"Please," I mouthed with desperation.

His hand slid over my ass and skated down to my inner thighs. I clasped my eyes shut, feeling every graze of his fingers. Every inch of movement brought me closer to the peak of arousal. I'd pleasured myself, but no one had ever touched me before.

A bent finger swept lower and brushed over the slick seam of my heat. My clit clenched in response, my nipples pebbled tight.

I was on fire, my hips pushing back and forth from the intoxicating need driving me insane. Goosebumps exploded over my flesh.

"I don't think you're ready for me," a whisper brushed over my ear.

Stiffening, I glanced over my shoulder to his wide grin. Was he blind?

"Maybe we shouldn't do this then," I suggested and started to shift as if to move away from him.

In response, he drove one finger into me, plunging deep.

I arched, moaning loudly.

"No, my mistake. You're ready," he said with a teasing sarcasm.

If I wasn't completely lost to him finger-fucking me, I might have thought of a smartass comment. Except, I barely breathed, barely stayed upright.

"Please don't stop." Never in a million years would I have guessed how delirious having a man touch me could leave me.

He released me, and I looked down between my legs to find him kneeling behind me, taking in all of me. "I've been thinking about licking this sweet, little pussy of yours since you walked into the bar."

My cheeks flared with fire, but I wanted him, and his growl confirmed he needed me too.

His mouth covered my arousal, licking and sucking.

I flinched at first, from the softness, the tickly sensation, the suddenness. At the pleasure rolling through me like waves on a beach.

He laughed softly, then slid his tongue over my lips, tasting all of me, leaving nothing untouched. Giving me long generous licks, I was left moaning for more. In response, he started to feast on me. The sounds were divine. He pushed his tongue inside me, the sensation incredible. I writhed beneath him as he tongue-fucked me, shattering me into a million pieces with the arousal he awakened within me. I shut my eyes, never wanting to come down from this high.

His teeth nipped at my flesh, causing me to cry out in surprise.

Breaking away, he moaned with pleasure. "You're fucking beautiful." He stood up and drew me by an arm to join him. His mouth and chin glistened with my juices. He licked his lips and wasted no time in dragging me into his arms.

Our mouths clashed, our kiss fast and starved. I tasted myself on his tongue and loved the intensity, the scent that screamed sex.

His hands fell to his belt, pulling at the buckle, then unzipped his pants. My hand slid down, our kiss never breaking. I wrapped my fingers around his shaft, hard as steel, covered in silk.

A growl came from his chest. He pushed my hand away. "No, you'll end this too fast," he hissed. With his large hands grasping the back of my thighs, he lifted me off my feet. He guided my legs around his hips. I dragged the fabric of my dress out of our way and the tip of his cock found my entrance with ease.

My heart leapt into my throat.

"So, are you sure about this, gorgeous?"

"Yes," I purred. "Fuck me already."

A savage hunger flared over his face, an animalistic look like he might lose control. Without ceremony, he pushed into me. I gripped his shoulders, feeling him stretch me, widen me. I cried out and squirmed against him. He held me tight, pressing my back to the wall and drove full hilt into me. The pain merged with plea-sure, both twisting into euphoria.

Meeting his green eyes, he groaned with desire. His hips thrust into me. I tilted my pelvis to meet every slap. A wicked grin spread over his mouth as he fucked me. As he unknowingly took away the one thing I had left. And I willingly gave it to this handsome stranger.

"Ahh." I floated on clouds, my heart racing.

He pumped into me faster and faster, filling me. The pain of having him inside me was always there, but mixed with pleasure, the ache eased.

"Come for me, gorgeous. Come all over my cock, squeeze me with that tight pussy."

My body responded to him, and I screamed as a climax ripped through my body. I pressed my face to the nest between his neck and shoulders to muffle my scream. In his arms, I convulsed while he kissed my face and neck.

"You are divine when you come."

When I finally breathed steadily and opened my eyes, I couldn't help but laugh. "That felt incredible." It didn't hurt anywhere near as much as I expected.

He held me close as he lowered me to my feet, slowly sliding out of me. Staring into his eyes, his gaze was brimming with lust, with frustration.

I lowered my skirt. "What about you? You didn't come?"

"Tonight was just for you." He pulled his pants up over his hips, then froze and stared down. I followed his gaze to the smear of blood on the tip of his still erect cock. He jerked his head up, his expression panic stricken. "Why didn't you tell me you were a fucking virgin?" He buckled himself up quickly.

His words surprised me, and it never occurred to me he'd find out, or care. "B-because it was my decision. And it wasn't a big deal."

He dragged me closer and nuzzled my neck. "If I knew…"

"What would you have done? Walked away from me?"

"Yes! Or at least gotten to know you better, taken you to a bed instead of fucking you against a wall. You deserved more than a stairwell."

Shaking my head, my chest already started to clench. "This was a one off. A night I'll never forget. And it was exactly what I needed. You helped me more than you'll ever know."

"Who in the world are you?" He cupped my face, his breaths raging. Our faces were inches apart. He stared at me with a cocktail of curiosity and anguish.

I softened against him, craving to stay with him. To run away from my real life. But I was fooling myself. Julian would hunt me down, and he'd kill this angel.

"A shadow is all I am. That's all you need to know." I pried myself out of his warm arms, and a chill quickly replaced his embrace. The need to stay plagued me, it tore at my chest, except our destiny wasn't meant to be.

My throat tightened, the ache between my thighs a delicious reminder of what he gave me. The relief was temporary, but he'd been exactly what I needed. There was no space for anything else in my messed up world.

Before I changed my mind and let emotions control me, I turned and ran toward the door and vanished from his life.

CHAPTER 4

*J*ulian was even more terrifying than usual this morning...if that was even possible. His eyes were hungry as he stared at me, and I knew he was imagining everything he was going to do to my body.

I shifted nervously, and I could feel the ache between my thighs from last night's activity, and it made me smile.

Wasn't he going to be disappointed.

"I hope that last night gave you enough time to get over your attitude. It will be much more pleasurable for you if you do it willingly. I'm a skilled lover," he said confidently, even though I couldn't imagine being happy with him in bed.

I didn't know much about the subject, other than last night, but I figured that an important trait to being called good in bed was being unselfish. And I couldn't imagine Julian ever being that.

He walked toward me, and I tried not to shiver under his gaze. He stood in front of me and trailed a finger down my neck, across my shoulder, and then down my arm.

And all I wanted to do was to get in the shower with scalding hot water and try to erase his touch.

It was time. It wasn't going to be pleasant.

But I didn't regret anything.

"I feel like I've been waiting forever," he whispered, heat glimmering in his eyes as he savored the feel of me.

I got up close to him, so close that I'm sure he thought that I was going to kiss him.

"You're going to be waiting forever," I whispered, not taking my eyes away from him.

He froze, not understanding what I was saying at first. And I watched as he got it.

All of a sudden, I was against the wall, choking from his iron grip around my neck. He sniffed the air, inhaling my scent, then let out a choking growl. He knew for sure I spoke the truth.

"Who?" he snarled. And the way he said it was one that I knew I would savor for a long time. It was the sound of someone who had been gravely disappointed.

I couldn't talk on account of his hands being around my neck, and I certainly wasn't going to give him Keon's name from last night, so I remained silent.

Which just infuriated him more.

"Tell me," he growled, squeezing my neck tighter.

At that moment, I wasn't sure if this was the end of me or not.

I had known that he wanted me, but I think I had underestimated just how much.

He finally realized that I wasn't able to talk and let go of me, pushing me to the ground as he pulled at his hair. He looked deranged, like he had lost all grip on reality.

It was spine-chilling. "I'm pretty sure I gave you warning that we were never going to happen," I said, admittedly unwisely.

"I'm going to kill whoever you were with last night. If you're lucky, I won't kill you. Who were you with?" he asked again, his eyes still wild.

"That's the great thing about the whole thing. I don't even know him," I said to him gleefully.

His eyes widened at the idea that I'd given my virginity to a stranger. I realized too late what was happening next, as his fist met my face.

There was an explosion of pain across my cheek. And then, everything was black.

When I came to, I was alone. But I could hear Julian's enraged voice as he yelled at someone. When I heard the soft placating voice who responded to him, I realized that he was yelling at my mother.

"How could you let this happen?" he hissed at her.

And I heard her pretty tears. The sound filled me

with an enormous sense of satisfaction that my mother's negligence of me all my life had finally come back to haunt her, even if I was now considered an adult in both the human and paranormal realms, and she had no real right of control me.

There was the sound of flesh hitting flesh, and then I heard her crumple to the ground as she erupted in sobs

Terrible or not, at the sound, a huge grin appeared on my face.

Hurried footsteps came into the room, and I quickly pretended that I was still out.

Obviously I didn't do a good job of it, because Julian's foot soon connected with my ribs.

"Get up," he growled at me.

My eyes flew open immediately. I was still alive, and although who knew what else he had in store for me, I figured that obeying him for now was probably the wisest thing to do.

I dragged myself off the floor, intensely aware of my splitting headache and the ribs that he probably cracked. If I still had my powers, I would've healed within just a few minutes.

As I was, I'd have to endure the pain for at least a day before any of my healing abilities would kick in.

It was all still worth it.

"I think you're going to regret what you did," he told me, his voice now eerily calm. He shook his head scornfully. "I know you don't care right now, but you will."

I highly doubted it.

"What are you going to do to me?" I finally asked after he just continued to stare at me maliciously.

His face broke out into a smile that was sinister looking, covering me in goosebumps. I knew that look would haunt my nights for a very long time. If I lived that long.

"I'm going to show you just how appealing being mine would have been. By the time you're done with what I have planned for you, you're going to be fucking begging me to take you back."

He grinned again, his smile wolfish like he was relishing the very thought of what he had in store for me.

A knock on the door sounded just then, and Alden, another of Julian's lackeys, appeared.

"The car's here," he said stiffly with a small bow.

"Excellent," he said, striding towards the door. He stopped at the doorway when I hadn't moved. "Come along," he said as though he was simply asking me to follow him for tea, instead of something no doubt ghastly and life-threatening.

My hesitation only made him happier. "I don't think you want to see what will happen if I have to force you to come with me." He sneered as he spoke calmly.

And despite my best efforts, a chill went down my spine. And all I could do was follow him.

We walked down the hall and out the door, where Julian's customary black town car was waiting. The drive was silent once we climbed inside, only making me more nervous.

To my surprise, we pulled up to the gate of his estate. After passing through the black, wrought iron gates, we drove for another ten minutes before we pulled into the circle drive in front of his manor.

I went to the open door, but he put his icy hand on my arm. "Stay here," he ordered before getting out of the car and walking inside.

For a second, I was tempted to get out of the car and try and make a run for it. But I would be no match for how skilled Julian and his coven were at hunting.

And I didn't want to find out what Julian would do to me then.

A few minutes passed, and he appeared again, holding a nondescript black box. I didn't dare ask him what was in the box.

But it was a strange thing because as we started driving again, all I could think about was the box. It felt as though the contents of it were casting a spell on me with an urge to tear open the lid and take whatever was inside. The sensation only intensified the longer we drove.

I sensed Julian's triumphant eyes on me, but I couldn't drag my eyes away from the box long enough to see why he looked that way.

Finally, after I had to literally put my hands under

my legs to keep myself from reaching out to take the box away from Julian, he laughed.

"It's really an interesting thing, Selena," he said amusedly. "Your power seems to call to you the same way that it calls to everyone else."

It took me a second, but then I gasped in horror. I bit down on my lip to make sure that I kept the frustrated scream welling up inside of me from coming out.

I knew what lay in that box. It was the very essence of me. The gold orb that contained the essence he stole out of me.

My power. He'd taken it away like a thief in the night. Now, I wasn't sure how to feel... A number of emotions rattled inside me. Most of all was fury, and I wanted Julian to hurt so much more.

"Why did you bring that with us?" I asked shakily. I watched, like a junkie who needed her fix, as he stroked the top of the box, watching me as I struggled.

"It's a gift for your new home. You know how I am about housewarming presents. I never visit someone empty-handed," he explained with a smirk.

"My new home?" I murmured, and he laughed at the fear in my voice.

Bastard.

"Now, I can't say any more...I wouldn't want to spoil the surprise," he said, and for the first time today, I wanted to cry.

Someday, I was going to make sure that I never felt this helpless again. I swore it.

The silence was deafening for the rest of the drive. At least thirty minutes passed before we pulled up in front of what looked like an abandoned office park. The building looked like it was set to be condemned any day, with cracks running throughout the aged, red brick walls, broken windows, and graffiti all over. A portion of the roof appeared to have fallen in as well.

It was a dump.

Julian stepped out, seemingly unperturbed about where we'd driven to. When I hesitated to follow him out, he threw open the door and grabbed my arm in a vice grip. He moved swiftly, like he couldn't wait to get to our destination. And he brought the box with him. My box.

I was nervous at this point, but also curious about where the hell we were. This seemed like the last place that someone like Julian would be hanging out, but the vampires were secretive, so what did I know?

Julian didn't hesitate, opening the doors and walking through as he dragged me behind.

To my surprise, we entered a modern office space complete with an attractive secretary sitting behind a front desk area.

What kind of magic was this? And what was in this office that was so important it had to be hidden like this?

The blonde stood up behind her desk as we approached like she was expecting us.

"Good morning, Mr. Morganstern," she said politely, sending him a simpering smile. "Ready for the trip?"

What trip was she talking about? I stiffened in Julian's grip, and he just clenched his arm tighter in response. I was definitely going to have a bruise after this.

"Ready as ever," Julian said flirtatiously, and I shifted uncomfortably, drawing an amused glance from him.

The receptionist, or secretary-—whatever she was—walked out from behind her desk, and I gasped a little to see that she appeared to be floating instead of walking. Although I could sense when someone was a paranormal, I actually interacted with them very little over the course of my life, at Julian's insistence. He was very controlling of his workers, or would-be workers, and so my only experience with other species came when the vampires held galas and the sirens not of age were sent to help with the catering of the event.

Whatever this woman was, I hadn't experienced her kind before. Which explained why I kept staring at her.

Evidently this was the wrong thing to do, because when she caught my stare, her entire countenance transformed in front of me in a flash. Instead of the beautiful blonde, what looked like a decaying corpse briefly flickered into view with what appeared to be worms where hair should be. Just a moment passed, and then the image disappeared and the blonde reappeared.

I took a step back despite Julian's grip, shock and quite frankly a bit of fear coursing through me over whatever just happened.

Julian laughed darkly. "They're going to think you were raised in a barn," he said silkily. "Banshees hate being stared at."

Banshees. Well, now I really wanted to get out of here. Banshees were demons you heard stories about around the campfire. Known for their deadly shrieks, they weren't something you wanted to run into and had actually been hunted in the past, dwindling their numbers. What was one of them doing here of all places?

"Sorry," I muttered, intentionally looking at the floor so that I didn't run the risk of offending her again. Julian just laughed louder, making me want to punch him.

I didn't keep my head down long as we began to walk down a dark, unlit hallway that seemed never-ending. The hallway somehow seemed to get darker as we moved farther down. The darkness brought with it a foreboding, suffocating feeling. My strength started failing me as we walked, muscles sore and exhausted. Julian was half dragging me by the time a tall door came into view.

There weren't any signs on the door denoting what lay behind it, but as the stark feelings intensified, I knew without a doubt that I did not want to see what was behind that door.

A sense of hopelessness washed over me, and even though I knew it was the byproduct of whatever dark magic was at play, I couldn't stop the tears from flowing down my cheeks. I put my free hand over my mouth as I tried to stifle the sobs that were threatening to come out.

Julian, for his part, somehow looked completely at ease, like the magic wasn't affecting him at all. How could that be?

The banshee opened the door, and that terrible feeling I had...well, it only intensified.

Because all of a sudden, I knew exactly what my punishment was, and Julian was right...I probably would be crawling back to him on my knees after this, if I even made it out alive.

Somehow, the doorway had led us to the place where I was sure that all bad dreams were born...Nightmare Penitentiary.

It was a place that had to be seen to fully grasp the horror it held. The door that we had walked through slammed shut behind us, and it was like we were standing in another world. Apparently that was what she had meant when she had asked if we were "ready for the trip," because we had left behind the sunshine of Chicago and instead were standing in a barren, grey landscape that looked like it had never seen the sun. The sky was a hazy, dark blue color, stained with clouds that resembled the sky right before a tornado struck. There were swirling, grey mists dancing around us, making it hard to see.

But you couldn't miss the black, wrought iron gates in front of us, the top of which was so sharp that it would impale anyone who tried to climb over them. There was barbed wire on top of the gate. Every couple of seconds, it sparked with something that I knew would hurt much worse than electricity. A simple metal nameplate on the fence announced where we were, but it was the feeling of terror that enveloped me as soon as I saw the gates that made it impossible not to know where we were.

Nightmare Penitentiary didn't have just one appearance. From the stories that I had heard ever since I was little, it had its own form of dark magic that allowed it to appear as whatever would be most terrifying to each individual inmate. It was the same with the cells inside. Since every magical creature was different, the cells were different in order to best contain its occupant. The dark, heavy, depressing feeling that I was still experiencing was something tailored just for me. As was the mausoleum feel of the outside of the prison.

I could say quite honestly that this terror I was feeling, I had never experienced anything like it.

And Julian knew it too.

The reason that he hadn't appeared to be suffering any ill effects was that he really hadn't been.

The gates creaked open in front of me, and it was all I could do not to bolt. Well that, and the fact that Julian was still holding onto me with a grip so strong that it felt like my bones were being crushed. The air felt heavy and thick around me, like right before the clouds broke in a thunderstorm. I was also sweating, but I didn't know how much of that was because of nerves.

"Julian, Nightmare Penitentiary?" I asked, struggling to keep the anger out of my voice. "Not sleeping with you shouldn't be the cause for going to a place where the worst criminals of the paranormal world are sent."

He just laughed bitterly. "I guarantee that there's nothing you could have done against your master that would've been worse," he told me. And then he began to drag me through the gates. At this point, I wasn't proud of it, but I began to struggle to get away. There was no way that I would survive in a place like this, especially without the full strength of my powers. The only thing a siren had in her arsenal after the vampires took their power was the ability to attract others to them. And the last thing I wanted was for a bunch of murderers and traitors to be attracted to me.

When I didn't stop struggling, Julian suddenly shook me so hard that my head snapped back. "Listen, little girl," he hissed. "I'm giving you a chance to be reconditioned. If you refuse this, then the only other option is for me to kill you. Is that what you want?"

Tears slid unbidden down my face. For a second, I actually debated it. Because the stories that I'd heard of this place...well, I didn't think I would be getting out of here alive anyway.

"I hate you," I spat at him.

He just smiled maliciously. "I'm well aware of that. But I think you'll be singing a different tune after a year in this place."

"A year?" I gasped, horrified. I had heard of murderers getting a month in here just because their experience was so wretched that they were cured for the rest of their lives, and justice had been satisfied.

Julian smiled again, just daring me to say something else.

He looked at his watch and sighed. "I have a meeting in thirty minutes that I can't be late for. So if you're done with your temper tantrum, we need to proceed," he said coolly.

I didn't answer him, but I'm sure that defeat was written all over my face.

Julian pulled me through the foreboding courtyard that separated the barbed wire gates from the main entrance of the prison. Now that we were in here, I could see that there were at least six guards dressed in all dark navy blue situated around the area. I couldn't tell what kind of creatures they were, because their crisp uniforms consisted of hoods that covered half their face. But the same heavy, cloying energy rippled over my skin, and I didn't have the strength or desire to look at them closer. I'm sure that the guards and I would be getting up close and personal over the next year.

From what I'd been told, the guards were put through a special program, essentially robbing them of compassion or any soul at all, making them incapable of being bribed or reasoned with as what occurred in most human prisons.

Of course, all the knowledge that I had came from rumors that I overheard at Julian's dinner parties, so I couldn't be sure of their accuracy. However, it was like you could feel the hatred emanating from the guards, like they already hated me on principle. I shivered, eliciting another smirk from Julian. I loathed him for enjoying this so much.

The front doors of the prison were just as menacing as the rest of the place. At least twelve feet tall and of solid black metal. The same sparks emanated all over it as it had on the front gates and the barbed wire.

A cloaked guard appeared next to us so suddenly and silently that I jumped in surprise. He held up his hand in front of the door, and it slid open with a screech like they hadn't been used in a long time.

I began to shake even more, because I couldn't see what was past the doors. Pitch black swallowed everything in sight. And one thing that I had always been scared of was darkness. Obviously, Nightmare Penitentiary was still working its magic on me, because Julian strode through the doors, still pulling me behind him, like the room was completely lit up.

I clung to Julian as we walked, even though the act made me want to vomit. The bastard chuckled and started humming, like we were at Disneyland or something. Like the hallway we had passed through to get to Nightmare Penitentiary, the air seemed to grow thicker and thicker as we walked, until the pressure felt so great that I was sure my head was going to pop.

I moaned in distress, and my body went limp as the pressure intensified. But Julian didn't let up. He just hummed and dragged me alongside him like a serial killer who'd just caught his victim.

The pressure increased until the pain was so bad that I thought I was going to die. And then, it suddenly evaporated.

A burst of cool air hit me the moment we stepped into a bright room. I squinted from the harshness of the light after the black void we'd just traveled through. The air carried a faint trace of cigarette smoke.

After a short pause, I slowly blinked rapidly so that my eyes could adjust. When my eyes finally recovered, I gaped at my surroundings, sure I had traveled somewhere far away from the halls of Nightmare Penitentiary.

I was standing in what almost resembled a giant library. I had once been inside the human's Library of Congress, and even that paled in comparison with the grandeur of this room.

The walls were covered in dark, walnut bookshelves, rows and rows of them lined every inch of the walls, stretching high above me...so high that there was a whole other level above me.

While some of the bookcases held books, most of them held an assortment of items that were no doubt of the magical variety. It seems like whoever's office we had just walked into had a little bit of a hoarding problem. There was a whole bookcase devoted to fairies. And when I say devoted to fairies, I mean that there were shelves of little fairies that had been captured in glass cases. Whatever was in that glass must've been crazy strong, since everyone knew that fairies were fucking powerful. They were also assholes, confirmed by the fact that at least five of them flipped me off when I happened to glance at them.

That was fairies for you.

Another row of shelves held bottles of various liquids, all different colors, and all glowing. One of them was even changing colors every few seconds. Interesting.

My observation of whatever collector's room I'd been taken to disappeared when I thought I saw a pair of eyes staring at me from the shadow in the corner. I gave a quick inhale of breath, but when I blinked, whatever I'd seen was gone. I moved slightly closer to Julian, remembering the age old adage that the enemy you knew was better than the enemy you didn't. Who knew what the shadows held at Nightmare Penitentiary.

I blinked again, and there was suddenly a man

standing behind the enormous dark wood desk that took up a large part of the middle of the room. As I looked at him, the edges of him seemed to slip in and out of focus, like black wisps of smoke… or shadows coming off of him. But no sooner had I experienced that thought than he came into complete focus, a wide grin on his too handsome face.

"Julian," he said in a voice that reminded me of a velvety night sky. He looked at us both, appraising me with a tilt of his head. I was trying to think of who he reminded me of. Besides the fact that he was scary as fuck, he definitely looked like someone I had seen before.

Suddenly I got it. He looked like that Tom Hardy celebrity that the humans were always going nuts over. Definitely a pretty face. Although I had a feeling that Tom Hardy wasn't nearly as menacing in person as this guy. The prettiest paranormals were always the scariest.

"Warden," said Julian, sounding almost respectful.

I looked at Julian in surprise. And then I looked back at the Warden with renewed respect and fear. Along with stories of Nightmare Penitentiary were always stories of its Warden. I heard he was some kind of demon. He had probably been that thing watching me from the shadows a moment ago. The rumors were that he fed off the prisoner's souls, dancing from shadow to shadow as they slept and he gorged himself.

Like I said...menacing.

"Is this my new friend?" he joked, and I could see the appreciation in his eyes as they traveled down my body. Unfortunately for me, I knew that someone like the Warden would be protected by the prison's magic from whatever energy I gave off that immediately had men begging to be my one and only. I also bristled at the mocking way that he said "friend." What an asshole.

I could tell Julian was torn at that moment. Part of him didn't like the way the Warden was looking at me, but the other part of him didn't want to tangle with a creature who didn't give two fucks that he was the leader of a large vampire coven.

Self-preservation evidently won out, because Julian gave a brisk nod. "I'm sure she will serve your prison well," he finally replied, a hint of a smile peeking out from his face. "She's just been recently broken in."

I flinched in horror, as I realized the connotation in his words. I wasn't just going to be imprisoned here. I was being sent to work here to service the guards or perhaps even worse, the prisoners. The Warden must have seen my terror because he grinned as well. "Well, she is pretty enough. I'm sure the boys will be very happy with her."

He sniffed the air, his eyes widening as he did so. "You brought me a siren, no less," he purred. "She must've really pissed you off for you to give up one of your special girls," he continued, his voice mild without any of the curiosity one would think would be attached to such a statement.

I saw a tic in Julian's cheek. I had no doubt that he was remembering my betrayal. Instead of answering the Warden, he presented the box to him. "A gift for you," he said, shooting me a satisfied smile.

The Warden's whole demeanor changed at the prospect of the gift. He opened it up like a kid on Christmas morning, and his eyes lit up as he surveyed the golden ball of light. I had been right. Julian had given him my power.

"That's mine," I growled, the words coming out before I could stop them. The Warden and Julian both laughed like I'd just told a joke.

"I've been searching for one of these for years," he told Julian appreciatively, his manner much more welcoming after the gift.

The list that I was keeping, the one of people I despised, one that had consisted so far of my mother and Julian...well, the Warden had just been added to it. And I decided right then and there that by the end of this year I would have my power back, or I would die trying.

The Warden took his gift and immediately went to a nearby bookshelf and pushed a few pieces aside to set it down as it continued to glow. I could feel it calling for me, and every piece of my soul wanted to answer its call.

He admired how the orb looked with his collection of oddities. Except, staring at the golden orb that seemed to shift inside like liquid gold, my heart clenched. Julian took my essence... my singing voice, where my biggest power lay. And he so easily gave it away to the Warden. I wanted to scream and collect what belonged to me.

The Warden once again turned back toward us, the movement so fast that once again, I could see how blurred the edges of his appearance were, until they sharpened once more.

"We have her for a year?" asked the Warden.

Julian gave a nod. "We'll see how much is left of her at the end of that year." He smirked, giving me a wink that set my teeth on edge. "I might not even want her back after your boys get done with her," he sneered.

The Warden smiled savagely. "Don't discount what the girls will do to her," he added, his face looking like the idea delighted him.

Sicko.

Julian looked at his watch again and cursed. "I have to go," he said to the Warden, who nodded in understanding.

Julian grasped both of my arms in his and gave me one last lingering look...I could see the longing in his eyes. I realized how much he still wanted me, and how much a part of him hated the fact that he was leaving me here. That longing disappeared after a second though, and all that was left was feverish triumph.

"Do miss me, darling," he purred, before he was out the door, leaving me with the Warden.

I trembled as I turned to face the Warden. Would he

demand that I have sex with him right away?

Much to my surprise, the Warden was busy examining my golden orb of power, sliding it around on his bookshelf like he was on some home organizing show. It was like I didn't even exist...which was not the usual reaction I got from males.

A few minutes passed, and I got tired of waiting. I just wanted whatever was going to happen to get over with. I cleared my throat, and he stiffened, apparently remembering I remained in the room.

"What are you going to do with me?" I asked in a resigned voice.

He grinned, and I shivered because I could see the promise of an eternity of torment in that smile.

"We'll let you get acquainted with your new home before you start your services," he said. He reached over and pressed a button on his desk, and then he went back to organizing his shelf, humming as he did so.

A minute passed, and then a guard appeared, dressed in the same uniform as the one's out front had been. Again, I couldn't see any of his features, due to the cloak that covered half of his face.

"Take her away," the Warden ordered without looking at either of us.

The guard strode towards me, and I was tempted to make a run for it...not that I would have anywhere to go. The entrance that Julian and I had come through had disappeared, and even now, standing in the middle of the room, I couldn't see any exits. Even the entryway that the guard had come through had disappeared.

The guard grabbed my arm before I could take a step and proceeded to march me towards the wall.

"Pleasant dreams," the Warden called after me.

I gritted my teeth to keep my body from shaking, because the way he said it sounded like a threat. That's all I needed was for the Warden to take a trip through my dreams.

Just as it seemed as though we might walk right into the bookshelf, an opening appeared and we were through the wall. Next thing, we were standing in a dark, cold corridor lined with cells made of the same black metal that had made up the outside of the prison. A scream ripped through the air, and I jumped.

The guard snorted at me.

I glared over at him. He didn't bother to respond to my glare, he just kept walking me forward. I was getting really tired of being dragged around.

The same oppressive feeling that I experienced before when I entered the Warden's office was also present in this hallway. I felt once again, like my energy was being sucked out of me. The guard of course strode along, seemingly completely unaffected.

The hallways were confusing. They reminded me of a labyrinth...and they all looked the same. It would probably be harder to find your way through the hallways and out of the prison than it would be to get out of your cell, if you were trying to escape.

The screams continued as we walked, and they were joined by a cacophony of moans and anguished cries. It sounded how I imagined hell would sound, with the dead bemoaning their fate. I honestly couldn't imagine hell being worse than this place.

I couldn't see into any of these cells. I didn't know if that was because it was lights out already, or if there was some kind of magical setting on them that prevented you from seeing inside. Either way, it was probably a good thing, since the sounds coming out of the cells were already terrifying enough.

As we walked, a tingling slid up my spine. It felt like someone was watching me. I glanced behind me, almost falling as I did so as I tripped over a gash in the concrete floor.

Looking back, I thought I saw someone slipping around a corner—another guard I assumed—and I tried to ignore my unsettled feeling.

I had spent a great deal of time in isolation, studying and training alone in my room. I was used to being alone, welcomed it even, as it meant time away from my evil bitch of a mother. But as we stopped in front of a cell so small that it could barely fit the cot that was stuffed inside of it, I felt more alone than ever before.

"Get in and change. I'll be back in five minutes. Don't make me have to help you get dressed," a gruff voice ordered, and I reluctantly walked inside, cringing as the metal door slammed behind me. I turned to ask the guard a question, but to my shock, he was already gone and there was nothing but darkness behind the bars in front of me.

I wanted to cry, but I held it in and turned to look at my new home.

As uncomfortable as the cot in my cell looked, I was just glad that it wasn't a bunk bed.

There was no way another being could fit into this room or on that bed, and that itself gave me a small bit of relief. I had assumed that I would be paired up with some dangerous lunatic, so a single occupancy cell was the best thing I had experienced all day.

A red jumpsuit was spread out on the bed. My new uniform I assumed. Remembering the threat in the guard's voice, I hurriedly slipped out of my clothes, trying to shield my body as I did so. I just hoped that everyone had an inability to see into the cells in this section and not just me. The idea of someone staring at me from the shadows was almost more than I could take.

The jumpsuit fit snug, but it seemed to do a good job of hiding my curves, something that was good, as I was desperate to garner the least amount of attention as possible.

True to his word, the guard came back a few minutes later carrying a tray of grey looking food.

He laughed when he saw my dismay and opened the cell door with a loud clang to grab my clothes and drop off the tray. I eyed the food suspiciously. It looked like congealed slop.

"Better get used to it, princess," he said mockingly, and it was all I could do not to scream at him. Of course, he could care less that I was in here under false pretenses. I'm sure that all of the prisoners claimed the same.

After sliding the food through, he left. Unable to summon an appetite, I curled up on my cot against the wall, allowing myself to cry for the first time since walking through Nightmare Penitentiary's gates.

The prisoners screamed and moaned around me. Some of their cries sounded angry, while others sounded broken-hearted. I could relate to both feelings at the moment.

I drifted in and out of sleep, too afraid to allow myself to drift all the way into dreamland.

I was fully woken up by the sound of chains rattling against the floor, and the rough barks of some of the guards. Standing up, I walked to the bars that separated me from the hallway and peered out to see if I could see anything. Unlike before, where all I could see was a black abyss when I looked into the hallway, now I could see what looked like four figures marching towards me, with another figure who appeared to be glowing in the center of them. The sound of the chains dragging on the floor got louder as they marched closer.

The four figures surrounding the glowing one were

guards, shrouded in their usual dark navy uniforms. They kept shooting glances at the person in the middle, the one that I could see now had chains around his wrists.

The one in the middle wasn't human, but he was in human form with shoulder length blonde hair that was so pale, it was practically white. The light surrounding him was so bright that it hurt my eyes a bit after seeing nothing but darkness the past few hours. It seemed to be emitting from inside of him, and cast him in a golden glow. His skin was a white gold color, and he was tall, taller than the guards around him. No wonder they were continually monitoring him.

He stared ahead of him as he walked, but I could see that his eyes were a brilliant blue, like the hottest part of a fire, that flickered and sparked.

A fae. That's what he had to be. I had seen a representative from the Light Fae Kingdom at one of Julian's parties. He carried this same glow, although I didn't remember it being this bright.

He was stunning.

But what was a Light fae doing in this place? The fae were powerful, and had their own laws and punishments that governed their people. I wouldn't have expected one of them to be here and not in their own prisons.

Unlike my uniform, his was a pale grey color, and he was only wearing pants. Despite my current situation, I couldn't help but devour the perfect ridges and valleys of his chest and arms. He was lean, but perfectly toned.

None of the group spared me a glance as they walked by, and I wondered again if you could see into the cells. Still staring at them, I gasped when the fae's back came into view. Unlike the pristine perfection of the front of him, his back was covered in what appeared to be a myriad of lash marks, many of them fresh ones, judging by the blood that was still seeping out of some of them. The new wounds were tangled with the scars of older ones. This poor creature was being tortured, and I let out a faint distressed sound at the thought. Was that same fate waiting for me?

At my sound, the fae's head whipped around, and our eyes met. Those blue flames seemed to burn even brighter as he stared at me intently, not breaking eye contact until a guard barked at him to stare ahead.

A lonely feeling crept into my heart at the loss of those eyes, and as his beautiful light faded, I felt even more despair about my situation. The screams of my fellow prisoners sounded even louder now, like they were mourning the fae's light as well. My screams would most likely join theirs tomorrow after my first day of "work." I shivered just imagining what horrors awaited me. I wasn't sure that the guards weren't worse than the monsters that could be found in these prison cells.

It was only nightmares that waited for me when I finally fell asleep.

CHAPTER 5

"Wake up," a voice barked as a hand was shoved roughly against my shoulder.

I flipped open my eyes, staring at the black stone wall inches from my face. That starkness and the groaning sound of someone behind me wrenched me back to my reality.

Nightmare Penitentiary was my new home for the next year.

I was trapped here. And today I would begin work as what amounted to a sex slave to the guards and whatever other demented, terrifying fiends the Warden deemed eligible for my services.

I was going to die, and no one would miss me. Terror clutched to my chest. I'd barely woken up, and already, I sucked in shallow breaths, hyperventilating.

The hatred I'd already felt for Julian was multiplied a hundred fold this morning, and I knew right then that I would do anything in my power to make him suffer. If I ever survived this prison, I'd make sure he hurt as much as I did.

"Get the hell up," a female voice growled. I glanced over my shoulder, blinking the sleep out of my eyes. A tall woman with wide shoulders glared at me, hands on her waist. She wore red prison pants rolled low on her hips and a short-cropped black tank top. Shadows crowded under her dark eyes, and my attention lifted to the stubs of black horns at the corners of his head. What was she?

I started to push myself up from the most uncomfortable cot in the world, my ribs aching, when something sharp pricked my palm. I pulled my hand back from the mattress to find a spectacular teal pyramid-shaped crystal. It glinted in the dull light like something swirled inside the stone. A beauty amongst the darkest of places.

Where had you come from?

A shuffling sound drew my attention to the top of my bed where a light brown mouse with a white face stared at me. Its little pink nose twitched, beady eyes locked to me, then lowered to the crystal.

"If I have to ask you one more time, I'm kicking you in the ribs. The Warden asked me to show you to the mess hall, now hurry the hell up."

My fingers quickly curled around the crystal as the mouse spun around and scurried away.

Shoving myself to my feet, I got up. I felt sore all over.

The inmate's eyes shone pure black, matching her short hair. Demon came to mind, and being this close with one scared me. I'd only heard tales about them having uncontrollable rage, but looking at her hard glare and the way her eyes narrowed on me, I didn't want to find out if that trait was real.

"Don't expect a welcome wagon every morning. You're lucky you get to leave your cell to eat. If you piss off the Warden, that will be gone. You'll have break-fast, then I'll take you to his office for your tasks. After that, I don't give a shit what happens to you."

My head still felt too groggy to really make sense of it all.

"Thank you," I offered.

She looked over at me, her lips pinched tight, frustration worrying her brow into a dozen lines. "Look, I remember my first day, and it fucking sucked. So I'll give you some quick tips. Then you're on your own, because we're not friends. Understand?"

I nodded.

"Don't start fights you don't intend to win. The scariest sonofabitch in this place is the Warden. And whatever you do, never say no to anyone who asks you for something."

My jaw dropped open at her words, but then again, could it be worse than offering these inmates sex? Well, unless they ask for my organs? I shuddered.

In truth, it took every ounce of strength to not fall to my knees and cry uncontrollably. I only had enough strength to find the energy to draw oxygen into my lungs.

Outside the cell, the communal area stretched out on either side of me. We headed to the right. Prisoners were everywhere, meandering, but most seemed to be going in the same direction. I stuffed the crystal in my hand into the pocket of my red jumpsuit.

Males and females openly shared this prison. The only discrimination made against us was us being supernaturals. While most seemed to hold their human form, I didn't miss the few who had long horns, a tail, one even a centaur, the bottom half of him a deep ale brown while long dark hair flowed down his bare back. He trotted up ahead, towering over everyone, most getting out of his way. I doubted anyone picked on him. One kick to the head, and they'd be dead.

The air smelled like it hadn't moved for years. Two walls of prison cells and dark concrete rose up on either side of me, three floors. The sheer enormousness of the building hinted at the large mass of people here. And this was only one compound of so many more in this penitentiary.

I didn't belong here. Not with creatures who'd violated the worst of the supernatural laws. Where the buildings looked worn and stained and a million years old. Where I was pretty sure we were right on Hell's doorstep. No windows to even show a hint of what it looked like outside.

This was a place where time would be immeasurable. This year would feel like it was stretching out for eternity, until I went utterly mad.

I was a little dramatic this morning.

My guide for the morning marched ahead, avoiding bumping into anyone, carefully selecting every step. Her fear was tangible, and she seemed to have worked out a specific way to survive. What was she in here for?

I somehow doubted she'd appreciate me prying into her business.

I still couldn't believe I was walking through Nightmare Penitentiary. It was legendary—and by legendary, I meant known for being the scariest place on the planet. Technically, I wasn't even sure where it was located.

Never in my wildest dreams had I imagined myself here. I wasn't a criminal... I just hadn't wanted to lose my virginity to Julian.

My heart rattled inside my chest as I sucked in sharp, shallow breaths. My head spun. I stumbled behind the girl's fast steps, keeping my head low, not daring to look anyone in the eyes. I wanted to be invisible and vanish.

I didn't have much experience with how my siren's ability to attract worked on other paranormals, but I doubted that being invisible was going to be an option.

The farther we walked, the more I noticed the other cells that were just as small as mine. Except most of them had three or four bunks with the same amount of prisoners crammed in there.

Somehow, I had gained a cell on my own, and I accepted the small blessing in this hellhole. Other cells had inmates still locked inside. They gripped their metal cells, leering out at everyone, yelling curses at us all. A man with a shaved head and black eyes met my gaze, his eyes widening as if sensing me. This was why I kept my gaze low, to try and go unnoticed.

He whistled and cocked his head back, calling me over.

I quickly walked away, not wanting anyone's attention. I made a mental note to steer clear of those prisoners. They were locked up 24/7 for a reason.

We entered a large room, walking past three guards in black, who were avidly and suspiciously watching everyone walking inside.

Stark white walls. Lines and lines of long tables and benches. All bolted to the ground. This was a school cafeteria on steroids. Inmates were everywhere, dressed in black and red prison clothes. The sound of chatter grew deafening. While the smell was anything but appealing, my stomach still growled for food after missing the last few meals.

My guide made a quick step to the right to escape from me, meeting up with two other girls. They hugged and chatted. When they all looked over to me, my skin crawled. I tried not to overthink it. I was the fresh meat gaining their attention.

Don't discount what the girls will do to her. The Warden's words haunted me. Could these women easily sense my siren side? Usually, my presence affected people, but most didn't know why or what was special about me.

As I stalked toward the end of the line for food, I tried to push those worries aside or I'd paralyze myself with fear.

There were three guards nearby, chatting to each other in low, rough voices. Cameras hung from the corners of the room along with what looked like lasers. Did they shoot anyone who caused trouble? They weren't messing around in this place.

Once I reached the counter, the cafeteria worker wearing a hair net shoved a tray into my hands with food already served.

"Next," she yelled, and the girl behind me shoved an arm into my back, sending me forward. I stumbled out of the way and turned to the room. Spotting a free table near the side wall, I walked over and slid onto the bench.

My heart beat frantically. I was completely alone and so far out of my comfort zone, I might as well be on Mars. I realized what a sheltered life I had led up until now. The prisoners around me were paranormals unlike any I'd been around before. Strong. Terrifying. Some covered in tattoos, others with mohawks. The demons hung near the entrance, all with cut horns. Apparently, there were cliques in prison, just like in the outside world, and the ones who looked similar stuck together. Made up of both male and females, these gangs filled the room. The more I looked around, the more I noticed that there weren't many loners like myself. I'd watched enough movies to understand the reason for forming a team. *Protection.* The few individuals completely alone kept their heads low and shoveled food into their mouths as quick as they could.

Gripping my plastic spoon, I looked down at my meal. Apple wedges, oatmeal, two slices of white bread, cup of milk, a dollop of red jam and a small cube of margarine. It was a step up from the slop the guard had tried to feed me the night before.

It had been so long since I ate food like this though in general. Mama starved me with salads to maintain a figure, making sure that I always looked perfect.

Wasting no time, I started eating. The food tasted bland. I didn't care though, and washed it all down with the milk. It put something in my empty stomach and distracted me for a few moments from the horror of this place. I had almost forgotten what bread tasted like. Now it melted on my tongue, and the margarine actually tasted a little bit like heaven in my mouth. I'd missed food.

A sudden piercing scream in the background had me flinching. The apple slice flipped right out of my hand and fell to the ground.

I twisted around, my pulse thundering in my veins.

Two men were hurling punches into another guy, pinning him into a cornered alcove. The spot was conveniently concealed from the three cameras in the room. The one spot of no cover, and they knew... apparently, they all knew the tricks and how to get around the system.

I twisted around to find the guards were conveniently gone.

Everyone watched the unfair fight, but no one cheered. They were conditioned to not draw attention to the cameras. No one went to stop them, not even those behind the counter serving food. My stomach clenched at seeing the brutality with which they ganged up on someone smaller than them. By some miracle, he slipped out from under them, his face bloody, his eyes bulging with dread. He saw death, and this whole room was about to watch him die.

I was going to be sick, my insides tightened as they threatened to give up the food I'd just eaten.

The limping man came in my direction.

I wasn't sure what to do.

Inches from him careening around my table, one of the brutes lunged after him, bringing the man down fast. He crashed down on top of him. The sound of his escaped breaths rattled out, cutting through the silence.

The attacker's eyes gleamed red, and his meaty hand grabbed the man's head before smashing his face into the hard linoleum floor.

A small cry escaped my lips as I pulled farther away, shoving myself along the bench as far from them as possible. My brain shut down as the crowds now burst into cheers.

Zap.

A crackle sounded. The hairs on my arms lifted.

One yellow laser beam lashed across the room. It struck the attacker's brow, sending him into fit. He convulsed violently, the man beneath him affected too, by sheer touch. The electrical current pulsed through them both.

My brain stuttered from the chill gripping my spine, from what I was seeing.

The explosion of shouts deafened me. But I couldn't take my eyes from the brute whose body seemed to be morphing. Twisting and stretching. Black fur exploded over his body, clothes falling off him in shreds. His face contorted, jawline extending outward.

He unleashed growls, his body thrashing. Froth dribbled from his mouth before he finally collapsed. His body giving out.

Where the huge man lay earlier, now in his place was an enormous black wolf, still on top of the victim, also passed out.

The animal was too big to be a wolf. Fur tangled. Fangs too long. Those red eyes. They seemed to pierce right through your soul.

He was a damn hellhound.

My breakfast hit the back of my throat. They were

territorial as hell and killed anything in their way. No sympathy. Everything to them was a massive hunt. Born of the darkest ashes in the pits of Hell, everyone feared them. Even vampires.

Cold sweat broke out over my body.

The hellhound's friend stepped closer, his head tilting back, unleashing a shattering howl that trembled the walls. He pumped a fist to his chest.

Oh fuck!

I scrambled to get out of there, when someone snatched my wrist and spun me back around.

The second hellhound had me in his grip. Black eyes encased by a red circle. Black hair pushed off his face, sitting messily around his rugged face. His gaze searched me. He stood over me, strong, formidable, handsome. I hated that I had that thought after what I'd just witnessed.

Still, I fixated on the tick of his jaw.

I stiffened my spine and managed to find my words. "Let me go. Please."

The corded muscles in his neck flexed while the hard expression on his face dissolved. It was replaced with a look of awe.

"Siren," he murmured. That heavy, dark voice tore through me, leaving me quivering.

Silence broke over the room.

Everyone was clearing out of the room in a mad rush.

I breathed in and out, but the air wasn't reaching my lungs. Fear pooled in my stomach.

His fingers unfurled from my wrist. "Go now, before the guards get you too," he commanded. "Run!"

He sounded like he almost cared. I had to be hallucinating. I spun just as half a dozen guards, armed with guns and shields stormed into the mess hall.

Tucking my head low, I somehow managed to bypass them and darted outside with everyone else.

Someone grabbed my arm, and a small scream flew past my lips. My heart thumped loudly in my ears.

I spun to see the woman from my cell this morning staring at me, and relief washed over me.

"Calm down, geez." She rolled her eyes like what just happened in there was an everyday occurrence. "Come on, I need to take you to the Warden."

I followed her amid the chaos, my pulse beating rapidly. In all honesty, if this happened all the time, I wasn't sure my heart could take it.

Still, my mind kept swiveling back to the hellhound and his words.

Siren.

CHAPTER 6

"Sit," the Warden commanded, his voice so smooth and menacing, there was no ignoring it. His gaze was glued to a laptop screen in front of him at his desk.

I slipped into the extravagant office from the doorway and sat in the leather chair across from him. Shelves of collectable ornaments filled the room everywhere. Thick black curtains partially covered a window to my left. Darkness winked back, but I sat too far to make out if that was night outside or simply an illusion. I had so many questions about this prison...like where were we? Was it true that the Nightmare Penitentiary was named by Hades? Were we close to the Underworld?

My attention flew to the nearby shelf with my orb. I felt it calling to me, the hairs on my arms lifting. Gold waves rippled inside the sphere like a restless sea. My heart tightened at the sight of what belonged to me. Just like everything else taken from my life, my songs were stolen now too. Julian had controlled every-thing… and now the Warden owned me for the next year.

Irritation stirred in my chest, but I said nothing like my mother had always taught me. *A lady is seen but not heard.*

"Nev, close the door behind you," the Warden snapped.

I glanced back at the girl who brought me here. Nev was her name. She met my gaze for a split second, but there was no help there. Only dread and the desperate need to leave the office urgently filled her dark eyes. The door shut behind her with haste, and I turned to face the Warden.

He had already lifted his gaze and was studying me. One thick eyebrow arched, lips thinning. In the dim light of his office, I swore black shadowy wisps shim-mered away from his body.

"How was your first night at Nightmare?" he asked, as though I'd spent my time in a hotel and he was inquiring about the comfort of my feather down mattress.

"I have my own room, which I'm appreciative for." At this point, I wasn't willing to anger him until I knew exactly where we stood. Until I figured out if I had any chance of making my life less hellish than it currently was.

Not many people had given me a chance in life to be anything but the daughter who had to listen. A girl who was owned. The student at the school who kept to herself. I had secrets I couldn't share. So I did the best with what I had given to me.

"Good, good," he murmured, not really caring what I said. "Now, let's make this quick. I had an agreement with Julian that you will provide a service to my guards and some select inmates. You may not realize this, but a visit with one of Julian's girls helps take the edge off most of my men. It reduces the violence tremendously. So to have you for a year living with us is fantastic."

Warning bells were going off in my head as my stomach tensed. I didn't want to be a relief to anyone in this place. My thoughts flew to the hellhound back in the cafeteria. He might kill me if I had to take him as a client. "I-I've never done this before. I-I don't think I can do—"

"I do not plan to throw you to the Wolves, Selena," he said with sincerity in his eyes, his shoulders softening. "There will be a schedule I will manage, and I can be fair if you do as I say."

I chewed on the corner of my lip, hating everything about this conversation. The more I thought about my task in this prison, the more my head spun and breakfast was going to come hurling out.

Taking a deep breath, I tried to tame my racing

heart, tried to focus on how to survive what he proposed. I knew this was coming, of course I did, but knowing and being thrown down into the rabbit's hole were two completely different things.

The heaviness of his gaze had me looking away, and my gaze instinctually swept over to my orb up on the shelf again. I'd lost my life and a part of myself. For so long, I went out of my way to not think about what was coming my way. I just needed to forget how messed up my world had become. On some delusional level, I never thought it would *actually* happen to me.

Unfortunately, the universe had no intentions of letting me escape my fate. And now, here I stood in the most dangerous of the supernatural prisons talking about my schedule for the sex services I was about to begin offering Nightmare Penitentiary's inhabitants.

"Maybe I just need a bit more time to acclimatize," I suggested, lifting my gaze to his dark one.

He was shaking his head before I even finished talking. "Don't upset me, Selena."

I stared at the Warden, held his intense gaze. Distrust flared within me. I hated that I never had any power in my relationships with those around me. That thought alone was enough to crush my spirits even more.

When he looked at me, it wasn't with the same desire I'd seen other men carry. I had zero influence on him, which put me in an impossible position.

He rose to his feet, towering over me. Heavy boots

tapped the stone floor as he rounded his desk and made his way to the shelves farther into the room. His long midnight colored coat snapped behind him with each step.

Reaching up to a shelf, he retrieved a long, white tail. He stroked it, looking at it while he talked. "I once had a nine-tailed fox shifter admitted to my prison for murder. While under my roof, we talked about what I expected from her like I do with every single inmate. Each one of them out there are given tasks. Well, my little fox thought possessing me to escape would be a smarter move." His head tilted up, those dark eyes glinting in the light.

I couldn't take my gaze off the tail in his hand, the one that must have once belonged to this poor shifter. Fear rippled down my spine. He'd never let me get away with anything but being his slave. I wanted to cry, and my eyes pricked with tears. This couldn't be happening.

He replaced the tail and strode toward the desk before collecting a piece of paper from under a pile of folders. "I have your schedule set up and ready to begin tomorrow."

"T-tomorrow?" I stuttered, my breath hitched.

"I will send for you to be collected. I have arranged for a special work room for you. I'll send for you tomorrow." He smiled like he was doing me a favor. But I wasn't benefiting out of this arrangement one bit.

Which was exactly what Julian had hoped by submitting me to this hellhole in the first place.

Fire welled inside me, my whole body trembling. My head wracked with finding a way out of this mess. Suddenly, I couldn't breathe. I shuffled to my feet quickly and curved around past my chair, my hip knocking into it in my rush. Then something popped out of my pocket.

Clank. Clank. Clank.

The pyramid shaped crystal I found in my bed now bounced over the stone floor. It hit the edge of the wall and settled down near the foot of a wooden cabinet.

Quickly, I rushed over and collected the crystal, having completely forgotten about the gift from the tiny mouse.

The Warden's heavy breaths deepened. "What do you have there?"

I curled my fingers across it, not wanting him to think I stole it on my first day. Would he believe me if I explained that a mouse brought it to me? I wouldn't believe me.

"It's nothing."

"Show me," he demanded, his voice climbing.

Reluctantly, I raised my hand and unfurled my fingers, revealing the teal colored crystal. My throat dried, stealing my voice.

His eyes widened, and something new slid over his expression. One of curiosity...and wanting. "Where did you get that from?"

"It was a gift," I admitted quickly, which technically was the truth.

His brows pulled together into one line, his gaze never leaving the crystal in my palm. "So, then you know the value of this piece and what exactly it means?"

I had no clue. "Of course, which is why it means so much to me."

His midnight eyes met mine, a hardness glinting behind them. The corners of his mouth quirked. While the nerve under one eye twitched.

He wanted this crystal. Just like the rest of his collected treasures, he eyed the beautiful stone. He counted himself successful based on what items he'd obtained… it was written all over his face. But the Warden wanted to play games, and that gave me an idea.

"Would you like this crystal?" I asked, lifting my gaze and closing my hand around the pyramid, stealing it from his sight.

He scrunched up his nose while his sight followed my every movement, like those videos of cats who all move at the same time following a fluffy ball on a stick. I may not be able to influence him with my powers, but I'd just uncovered the Warden's weakness.

"You'd part with something so precious?" he asked, his head tilting to the side.

I shrugged. "At a price, isn't everything for sale?"

It didn't take long for his demeanour to shift back

to the hard-assed Warden, eyes narrowing at me. He didn't say anything more.

"If you're not interested, that's okay." I pushed the crystal back into the pocket of my jumpsuit. "I better head back to my room then." I turned, while my skin pricked with goosebumps. *Play hard to get,* my mother always said. *Men will never be able to resist a girl saying no to them. They are wired that way inside. Needing what they couldn't have before anyone else.*

The Warden's stare weighed heavily on my back as I crossed the room.

"You know I could just take it from you?" he muttered as I reached for the door handle.

"I don't think you will though," I answered him smugly.

There was a pause. And then... "What's your price?"

Without turning around, I answered, "Change my job for the next year at Nightmare Penitentiary." I couldn't bear to look at his face and see it contort and twist with disapproval. I stared at the black door, which on my arrival to the prison hadn't existed in his office. Must be an invisible door.

Waiting for his response was excruciating, but this had to work.

The rip of paper had me turning around. He was shredding my schedule, and my heart leapt. If I saw that mouse again, I was going to kiss him. He'd just saved my life by bringing me a random gift. Maybe fate had decided to throw me a bone after all and save my ass.

"Agreed," he rapidly growled, tossing the ripped pieces of papers into the trash can. "This stays only between us. Julian is to never find out. Otherwise, the next task you will be appointed will be serving the monsters down in the lower pits of Nightmare. And if that happens, you will never be the same again. Understand?"

I nodded my agreement fast, swallowing past the lump in my throat.

"Your job here for the next year will be to deliver meals to prisoners in their cells." He rounded his desk and closed the distance between us in three long strides. Eagerness twisted his expression, reminding me of Golem from The Lord of The Rings.

I stood tall, lifting my chin to face him. "But aren't meals served in the mess hall?"

"Not everyone is permitted to leave their cells, and we have many times when everyone is served food in their cells. I change the schedule a lot to keep everyone on their toes. Now, give it to me."

I drew my hand out of my pocket and opened my fist. Then I rolled the beautiful stone onto his open palm. The moment it touched his skin, a moan slipped past his lips, and then he licked them.

Sickness churned in my gut to see the hunger with which he took the crystal. He swept away from me, his head low as he studied his new toy, and tossed over his shoulder, "You can leave now."

I did just that, and hoped to the goddess that I wouldn't regret giving him that stone. That Julian would never find out. I stepped out of his office, closed the door behind me, and made my way back to my cell followed by a guard that had been waiting outside.

I had a tiny little mouse to thank for saving my ass. Literally.

CHAPTER 7

"You're in the maximum security section today," said Alessia with a shiver.

Alessia was on the service staff with me. She had been sentenced to five years for killing a werewolf at a party when he wouldn't listen to the word "no." His pack had demanded retribution as the werewolf happened to be the Alpha's nephew. So here she was.

Evidently, vampires weren't the only assholes in the paranormal world.

"Is that bad?" I asked, nibbling on my bottom lip worriedly. It was my second day serving food and so far, it had been relatively easy despite the fact that the rest of the prisoners didn't seem to have the same defense to my powers as the Warden did. It really was unfortunate that I didn't have an off switch to the one ability I had left. It would have come in handy in a place like this. These were not the kind of men that I wanted to be attracting.

"Just don't look any of them in the eye," she said soothingly. "The guard will be standing next to you while you push the tray through the gate. There's some kind of spell that allows for things to go into their cells but not to come out. The prisoners won't be able to touch you."

I shivered involuntarily and nodded. The last thing I wanted to do was to get the attention of the prisoners in that section. There were several maximum security areas in the prison. From what I'd heard around the kitchen, no one actually knew how large the prison was. There were several levels, and from what I gathered, there were some areas of the prison that made this one seem like Disneyland. Not that I really knew what that meant. My mother hadn't been the type of woman to take me to Disneyland, even if Julian had allowed her to.

But I still understood the expression.

A guard was waiting for me right outside the kitchens as I pushed my cart out into the hall. Somehow, the carts never ran out, and I never had to come back to the kitchens to refill-—just another of the magical mysteries of Nightmare Penitentiary.

I couldn't see the guard's face, thanks to the hood that covered most of it, but he seemed familiar to me. Maybe I'd been assigned to this guard before.

"Hello," I said politely, hoping that he would respond if he'd seen me before.

I was met with silence.

Okay then…

I followed him down the hall. He stopped in front of a bare, grey stone wall. We waited for at least a minute before I opened my mouth to ask him what we were doing. Before I could get a word out, the wall disappeared in front of us, and my mouth opened in shock as a drawbridge over what appeared to be a flaming sea of lava was stretched out before us.

The smell of sulfur grew thick in the air, and I could feel the heat of the lava threatening me.

The guard began to stride across the bridge. He didn't look back to see if I was following him.

I was frozen in place. There was no way I was going across that bridge. It was swinging as he walked across it. Knowing my luck, I would either send the cart or myself, spiraling down to its fiery depths if I tried to cross it.

He finally realized that I wasn't following him, because he stopped and turned around. I could practically feel the weight of his disgruntled glare, even though I couldn't see his eyes.

I took a hesitant step onto the bridge, after he strode back towards me, a little afraid he was going to throw me in the lava anyway if I didn't start moving. I drew in a hiccuped breath when the bridge swayed as I began to walk across it. Mercifully, the guard stood still, watching me from his vantage point halfway across.

I couldn't look at the lava below me, or even watch the bridge underneath my feet. Everytime I tried to do that, I was once again paralyzed in place. Instead, I kept my eyes on the guard, whose face I still couldn't see. Step by step, I made my way towards him. As I got closer to him, he began to walk backwards, not turning to look where he was going. I couldn't see his eyes, but I know they were on mine. In that moment, it felt like we were on the same side, no longer guard and prisoner. I wasn't alone.

Before I knew it, I was suddenly across. I ignored the strange urge I had to throw myself in the guard's arms in thankfulness. I'm sure he wouldn't appreciate that.

He surprised me by giving me a few minutes to recover from crossing the bridge, which I needed since my insides felt like jello after the adrenaline rush. Taking a few deep breaths, I gave him a small nod, and he turned and began to walk away.

We stood in front of another seemingly blank wall. This time, he took out a small knife and made a slash on his hand. Squeezing his hand so some of the blood dribbled out, he wiped it on the wall. The wall absorbed the blood, and then it opened with a loud groan.

I gasped and jumped back. Hadn't these people heard of a thumbprint reader? Was a sacrifice of blood really necessary? I shuddered, even knowing that most likely, the guard's supernatural abilities would allow him to heal quickly.

I hurried after him through the entryway, afraid that I would be trapped in this room forever if I strayed too far away from him. I heard that Nightmare Penitentiary acted like a sentient being, constantly changing its rooms as it saw fit. It's what made it impossible to escape from it.

After walking through a dark tunnel, one that creeped me out since I swore I could feel eyes watching me the entire time, we emerged into another long hallway, lined with cells. I was surprised after the dramatics of the journey that it didn't look too different from my section of the prison.

Nightmare Penitentiary wouldn't need anything too outwardly fancy though. I learned that every cell was spelled to provide the maximum amount of security needed to imprison that specific supernatural prisoner. Since every supernatural was different, security needed to be different as well. While silver bars might keep a werewolf contained, it would have absolutely no effect on a vampire. I wondered what kind of special features the cells in this maximum security area held.

I had a feeling I didn't really want to find out.

I was expecting hideous monsters in these cells, so when the first cell we stopped in front of a solid iron door with a slot to leave food and a window to look inside of. When I peered inside, there was a seemingly normal looking young woman with orange and yellow ombré hair cascading over her shoulders, and I was a little shocked. It was dark and so lonely in there, my heart went out to her.

Her attention fell on me as I looked through the door slot at her. Her eyes widened with a happy surprise. "UberEats? I placed my order ages ago. Not a good way to earn a tip."

A smile curled on my lips, and I liked this girl immediately. "Sorry. You gave me the wrong address," I teased.

With a mock-forehead slap, she across her cell toward me. "Of course! I forgot to put 101 Naughty Corner Solitary Avenue."

Dressed in gray prison scrubs, she moved closer. "Happens all the time."

She smiled so easily like nothing in the world could touch her. Except she was in solitary confinement. That would drive anyone insane.

Pushing herself on her tiptoes, she studies the food options on my cart. "I guess...the plastic-wrapped sandwich, a bruised banana, the bag of crushed chips, the stale cookies, and some room-temp bottled water. Except, multiply that order by five," she instructs and glances up at me with a vulnerability behind her gaze. "Solitary makes me hungry."

I laughed. Her jokes were refreshing in a place that

wore me down. I started handing her the items through the food slot the guard had opened up for me.

"What did you do to end up in here?" she asked me. "You seem…not terrible. Not like some of the others I meet down here, anyway."

She glanced over to the guard standing behind me before answering. "I just joined in on a prison yard fight, turned into my beast, and knocked over some guards," she rattled off with a shrug as she placed her food on the floor of her cell. "What about you? How'd you get put on food duty?"

"Just lucky I guess," I offered her a smile, thinking back to how lucky I was to have the crystal brought to me by my little mouse friend.

"What are you?" the girl finally asked me.

"Late," I answered. "I gotta go back to the other level to deliver more food. See you around." I pushed my cart away, one wheel squeaky.

"Wait, what's your name?" she murmured.

I turned to face her. "Selena. You?"

"Sinclair."

She studied me intently as though she sensed the real me for the first time. The corners of her mouth curled upward. "Oooh, I see what you are now. You work it, girl… it's getting hot in here," she purred, teasing me as she offered me the sexiest look any girl had ever given me.

I couldn't help but laugh at her compliment. I could

see myself getting along well with her very well if she was in the main compound with me.

"Nice to meet you, Sinclair. Don't eat all that in one sitting." I hurried ahead to my next delivery.

"Oh, one more thing," she called out, and I glanced back over my shoulder.

"I'm a huge, huge fan of pop rock candy. If you see any, do a girl a favor."

"Of course," I said.

The guard and I moved along to serve more inmates. I was almost done with my round of dinner deliveries and was contemplating how bored I was going to be tonight in my cell, when I happened to glance at the last prisoner that I was about to serve. A hulking beast of a man stood up as I approached, and holy shit… My brain short-circuited.

My body was instantly awake and at full attention. He was huge. Tall, broad shoulders, and cut—like a Greek statue. His movements were a graceful stalk, like a predator in the wild, a rolling glide of muscles. Whoa… Before my brain could process anything else, I felt myself responding to him on a primitive level, turned on in a way I had never experienced before. My heartbeat sped up, my breathing turned shallow as images of him touching me intimately raced through my mind, graphic images of this mountain of cut muscle defiling me.

What the hell? What kind of supernatural was he? Because I had never felt like this before.

He had to be doing something to me. Right?

There was a crazy surge of hormones and chemicals telling me I belonged to this man. I was shocked by my body's near-violent response and the man I was seeing before me, too shocked to do anything but watch him. His well-defined traps, pectorals, and biceps, rolling and shifting under his thin, deep orange uniform, gave hints at what else lay beneath.

Outlines of thick, muscled thighs were displayed inside his prison issued pants, which were hanging low on his hips. His outfit was complete with the scuffed black boots he hadn't bothered to lace that all the prisoners were forced to wear in this section of the prison.

Crime had never looked so sexy. My insides clenched as my eyes slowly traveled back up that body to those muscle-rounded shoulders and his defined neck, imagining everything a body like that could do. Crap.

He was beautiful. His hair was a little overgrown, but it looked good on him. Really good. His black tresses fell into his eyes as dark brows and dark stubble accentuated his chiseled face. He had that I-look-this-sexy-naturally look. And I had a feeling he did... First thing in the morning, without having to do anything. If ever there was male perfection, it was him.

That body combined with his sculpted face was overkill. Completely unnecessary. He was the living embodiment of primal, raw masculinity. He put my fantasy guy—the perfect man I had assembled in my mind, the one who just the thought of made my blood pressure spike, the one who didn't have a chance of actually existing—to shame. And he was no more than five feet away from me now.

Tall, muscular, and beautiful, with just enough ruggedness... He paused in his stride, his focus landing on me. My breath caught as my heartbeat picked up. His eyes, a gorgeous steel grey color, were penetrating. They narrowed slightly and slowly raked over me, pausing here and there in their perusal. His attention was blatant and intense and paralyzing, and I felt self conscious as I nervously adjusted my uniform.

His expression was fierce, and the energy he threw off was impossible to ignore. Magnetic. Pulling me in. Something low inside me tightened in response. He took a step toward me, his predatory eyes jumping between my face and body. It was like being confronted by a large, wild animal, and it was the most intense experience of my life, terrifying and arousing beyond belief. A nervous excitement built inside me. Goosebumps ran along my flesh. My heart beat wildly as my chest tightened. I tried to control my breathing— aware a heaving chest might be a little too obvious, and also aware of the prison guard that was watching closely to make sure that I did my job just a few feet away.

My body was heating up everywhere his gaze lingered. I felt... Exposed. Vulnerable. Out of control. And I didn't like it. Finally, his eyes met mine. Wow...

Those eyes were piercing through me. Mesmerizing me. I was aware that I needed to look away, that I should, but his heated gaze drew me in deeper. Something clenched hard in my chest as those grey eyes bore into mine. I felt a dangerously strong pull to him, like a moth to a flame. Instinctively, I wanted to run away from it. From him. I had never seen a more attractive man in person. Definitely never had such a strong physical reaction to one, not even the guy from the bar. He was nothing like any of the paranormal creatures that I had ever seen before. He was tall and beautiful and manly. He had to be six three or six four in height. And those muscles. He had enough muscles to make me feel petite and delicate and feminine.

I had met many attractive men, the vampires unfortunately all had that quality about them, but none held a candle to him, and it wasn't just physical. He had a raw, intense energy; a savageness rolled off him, only magnified by his beauty. He was unlike any man I had ever met. Anywhere. Tearing my eyes away, I focused on preparing his tray, placing the napkin and spoon beside it while I tried to calm my racing heart and raging libido.

I could feel his eyes on me like a possessive hand. I couldn't even hide behind the veil of my hair, having been required to pull it into a ponytail earlier so my hair didn't get into the food. I tried to block out his intense gaze, which was quickly making me feel trapped, but I couldn't ignore it when he walked slowly up to the front of his cell so that he was standing right in front of me.

The heat from his body caressed mine. It was intimidating and arousing.

What I was feeling felt almost primal. It felt deeper, like some primitive mating instinct.

Get it together, I admonished myself as I shakily grabbed his tray from the cart I had been pushing and started to nudge it into the cell.

Was I actually sweating? Because it was either that or the temperature in the prison, which always ran freezing, had been turned up about five hundred degrees.

A few minutes later, I was still standing in the same spot in front of the cell, trying to get my raging heartbeat under control, mentally berating myself for the bizarre, deer-in-the-headlights response to the hot prisoner.

Realizing my hands were trembling, I quickly backed away and put them on the cart, desperate for something to hold on to and hoping it would help hide how rattled I was. Taking deep breaths, I attempted to calm myself. A static-electric-like hum started spreading all over my body. The hair on the back of my neck stood up. It was getting stronger the longer I tried to ignore it.

He was still staring at me. He hadn't bothered to pick up the tray I had pushed into his cell, not that I blamed him for that. I was pretty sure that they served slop to the prisoners in this area. Slop like I was served my first night.

I tried to calm my racing heart, to get myself to move, but the energy engulfing me was overwhelming.

Just breathe. Be casual. For heaven's sake, don't stare again! As casually as I could manage, I tried to start walking away. But I couldn't resist one more look back.

His half-lidded gaze was penetrating. It felt like he could see right through me. All my secrets. My damaged soul. And that scared the crap out of me.

Unable to handle the intensity of this man any longer, my eyes quickly darted away, breaking eye contact, only to land on his mouth. A very kissable mouth. Soft, sculpted lips. I couldn't help but wonder what they would feel like against mine. Soft and giving, or firm and aggressive?

He smiled, like he knew what I was thinking. His smile only made him more attractive since it softened his features, making him seem less menacing.

Despite everything inside of me that was pushing me to get closer to him, I finally dragged my eyes away and began pushing the cart again, practically running to get away.

It was only my imagination that the guard who was watching me seemed to growl as I passed by. Or that I could feel the prisoner's gaze on me long after I had left his sight.

I was definitely not going to be bored tonight in my

cell. The image of that prisoner wouldn't be leaving my mind anytime soon.

I ignored the part of me that felt desperate to see him again.

It was a good bet that I would be volunteering to serve this section of the prison again.

CHAPTER 8

A few days passed, and I had convinced myself that there was no way my reaction to that prisoner had been real. Men that hot didn't really exist. My mind had obviously been tripping, and I didn't have the luxury of losing my concentration in a place like this. I needed to forget him.

In passing, Alessia had mentioned a library in the prison. That one word had me buzzing, because it offered my mind a chance to escape. To let the words carry me away, to forget the precarious spot I landed in.

Back home, I read most nights to escape the reality of my world and pretend that even amid the darkest events, somehow, things would work out. Mama often called me naive, but some nights it was the only way to get through the darkness crowding in my head.

Pushing aside those thoughts, I traveled down a

long hallway toward the library. Guards stood at one end and more at the other end. Cameras followed our every move in this section, a passage that made for an easy spot to ambush someone if left unwatched.

I'd barely been here a few days, and already, I thought about dangerous paths and where it was easy to jump someone. Suffice it to say, if I got out of here, I was definitely not going to be the same kind of person as when I'd entered. .

Other inmates brushed past, nudging into my shoulder. Keeping my head low, I moved quickly.

But their eyes were on me... I felt them. Mostly the men, trying to catch my attention. The girls ignored me... for now anyway. But I knew the drill. Once word spread about what I was, the women would toss hate my way. I loathed the jealousy. For one, I couldn't control the influence I had over others without even trying. Second, what happened to women supporting women?

Swinging right at the end of the long corridor, I followed the sign on the wall toward the library. I stuffed my hands into the pockets of my prison pants and walked briskly down a brightly lit hall. Farther ahead, two enormous wooden doors stood closed, making me feel more of a dwarf in comparison. Snakes were carved into the dark wood, and black door handles waited to be used. A tinge of excitement pooled in my gut at what the library could look like if the doors were anything to go by. Maybe I'd spend every spare moment I was allowed here to pass the next year.

There were no other doors nearby, and the sign pointed this way to the library, so I guessed this was the right place. I remembered that Nightmare had an ability to reveal itself differently to everyone, so it could be just me seeing these impressive doors. *Please let the inside be just as stunning.* In my mind, I pictured rows and rows of bookshelves made of dark wood, ornate ceilings, and that heavy gothic feel from an old library. I knew I'd be disappointed, but a girl could dream.

Footsteps quickly closed in behind me, and I shuffled aside to let them pass, but so did the echoing steps.

I glanced over my shoulder, my heart beating faster at having someone coming up behind me that quickly.

"Hello, pretty little thing," a man droned as he leered at me, standing too close for my liking. Hair black as the night was slicked back. His skin and lips pale. Red veins streaked the whites of his eyes. When his mouth parted, fangs slipped out over his lower lip, and he feverishly licked them.

Sickness swirled around in my stomach. It seemed as though I looked straight into the face of a demon, except this was a vampire. Close enough, in my opinion. Except, this vamp looked sick. He twitched and wasn't blinking at all, and he didn't have the otherworldly handsomeness that Julian and the rest of his coven had either.

I glanced around to find no guards or cameras. Just me and this sicko. "Look, I'm not interested," I said shakily.

He lashed out and snatched me by the arms before shoving my back up against the wall. "I never asked if you're interested." Drool seeped out from the corner of his mouth.

He stood like a mountain over me, his fingers iron around my arms, holding me in place. As much as panic strangled my chest, I had to use my wits to survive.

I swallowed hard and blinked at him. Then I forced a smile on my lips. Drawing on every inch of bravery I had, I pushed out the sweetest voice. Behind it flowed the surge of my limited power. "I think you should step away from me now." My voice streamed. Energy pricked down my arms. If I had the power of my song, he'd flinch away in a second.

But the vamp just stood there, dumbfounded and confused like he'd suddenly forgotten the English language. My remaining ability had no influence over this crazed vampire. And I knew then how much shit I'd just landed in... I'd seen this look before.

Starved.

Ravenous.

Deadly.

Fuck!

He was overcome with bloodlust. And nothing could influence a bloodsucker in such a state.

Then… he attacked.

It happened so fast, I couldn't make sense of it at first.

Claws ripped down my arms, and I screamed.

He twisted one of my arms behind my back. His face shoved so close to mine, I sucked in the smell that lingered around him… That stale scent. Then he hurled me across the hall, and I was flying, my scream rushing past my lips. I hit the wall with the back of my head and somehow managed to stay on my feet as stars danced in my vision.

Fear flared over me. The fiend whipped in my direction, all crazy-eyed and wild. I wasn't a fighter, but my fists clenched. He barreled into me, his face smacking into me. I accidentally bit into my lower lip, ripping it open as I fell and hit the ground fast and hard. I barely had time to react.

I writhed against him, punched and kicked. Panic swallowed me. All I cared about was getting him off him. But when his hand clasped over my throat and pinned me down, dread closed in around me.

Jerking my head up, all I saw was this monster and my death in his eyes. I never stopped fighting while my lungs yelled for oxygen.

Darkness surged through me, growing, festering like a virus.

I knew things would be horrendous in prison. I knew I'd be in danger. But I wasn't ready for this. I'd at least expected guards to be around 24/7, and for the prisoners who were truly dangerous—like this one—to be kept in their cages.

His body was heavy on top of mine, and he made this disgusting hissing sound. Releasing his chokehold, he wrenched my head to the side, exposing my neck.

The predator pinning me down bared his teeth.

Terror collided with me about what would come next.

I went ballistic, fighting him as best I could. Thrashing against him, I screamed.

In a flash, he was flung off me.

I scrambled backwards, my brain and body numb of feelings. Crouching against the wall, I stared up bewildered. A guard dressed in black and wearing a hood wrenched the vampire away by the scruff of his neck. But the fuckhead swung around and launched at the guard.

They broke into a vicious battle, hitting the ground hard. Arms. Legs. Punches. Snarls.

My heart raced while my head swayed. I'd never seen a guard fight with his bare hands before. They always used weapons.

Rolling on the ground, the guard straddled the vampire before slamming fist after fist into his face. He was unstoppable, moving with supernatural speed. What exactly was he that he could overpower a blood starved vampire so easily?

The loud snap of bones reverberated from the fight. Next thing, the vampire was flung across the hall. He slammed into the wall and crashed down to the floor. Unmoving. Was he dead?

I could only hope.

I sucked in sharp, ragged breaths, my eyes glued to the guard.

He lifted his chin in my direction, the hood he wore now pushed off his head. Shadows danced over his face… I somehow knew that this was the guard who had been with me earlier during my food delivery to the maximum security sections.

Except staring at him now, able to see his face, a familiarity struck me. I'd seen him somewhere else too.

"Did that fucking rat bite you?" he asked in a deep baritone voice that left me buzzing.

I shook my head mechanically and blinked at him, studying his strong features, striking cheekbones, dark hair messy like he'd just dragged himself out of bed. Striking haunted green eyes met mine, and something in my mind clicked.

Oh. Fuck. I did remember him. It couldn't be.

A gasp fell past my lips. "Keon?"

Fuck!

The last time I saw him was at the bar on my last night of freedom. It felt like a lifetime ago, even though it had just been a few weeks.

I lost my breath. And all I could picture was him pulling out his large cock before he took me up against the wall in the stairwell.

He didn't speak right away but stared at me like he

waited for me to get over my shock. Except, my heart was plunging right through me.

Then he laughed, eyes wrinkling at the corners when he did. "You remember me now?" That deep sexy voice drew me out of my frozen state, and I frowned at him.

I felt all the blood drain from my face. I wasn't supposed to ever see him again. He was my one-night stand, the man who took what I refused to give Julian and didn't ask questions. And now, he was in this prison with me and had just saved me from a crazed vampire.

His body slid closer to me, his large presence making me aware of how much smaller I was next to him without my heels. I was no fool to ignore how incredibly built and stunning he looked in his crisp dark uniform. How those broad shoulders slanted down to a narrow waist, how my mind kept flashing back to our first encounter at the bar.

I'd had sex with this stranger, and now he stared at me like he pictured me bent over with my skirt shoved up to my waist.

My cheeks burned... in fact, my whole damn body burned, now that I really paid attention to him.

"All that blood on you suits you," he said nonchalantly. "It brings out your eyes."

I glared at him, wiping the back of my hand across my busted lip. Nerves clung to me. "You often pick up girls covered in blood?"

That stunning grin split his mouth, his white teeth on show. The corners of his mouth curled upward deviously. "If I remember right, you did the picking up."

Sweat collected at the small of my back, my pulse pumping fast through my veins. Suddenly, I was breathing hard like I had been back at the bar before we had sex. That anticipation of being with him left me burning up with heat again. My gaze fell to his full lips, remembering them on me. A tingle zapped through me and dove to the deepest pit in my stomach. All I could picture was me pinned to the wall, my legs wrapped around his hips. Maybe it was pathetic to think that was the hottest sex when he'd been my first and I had no one to compare to. There's no way it was really as good as I remembered.

I shook my head free of the fog, coming back to where I was and who stood in front of me. "You work here?" I felt stupid the moment the words fell past my lips. I sighed. "Well, of course you work here. Look at you in that uniform." My eyes slid over how his clothes fit perfectly over that sexy body I wished I'd spent more time exploring in the stairwell. I was burning up just remembering our time.

"How'd you end up in here?" Up close, he studied me as if searching for something on my face and neck.

I tilted my head back, chin high. "What are you looking for?" On purpose I ignored his question, not ready to talk about my shitshow of a life that led to me being dumped in this place.

"Looking for cuts and bites," he answered. "Vampires tend to go for major arteries on your neck for quick access to fresh flowing blood." He gently pushed the strands of hair off my face and over my shoulders. Soft hands traced my neck. His thumbs stroked the length of my collarbone, feather soft, leaving me trembling under his touch. There was something intimate and almost dominating about the way he searched my neck.

I sucked in a breath at his touch, trying to steady the desire coiling tight in my gut. "Thanks for saving me." I pointed my chin in the vampire's direction and drew away from Keon's reach before I did something insane like asking him for a repeat of the scene in the stairwell. "You killed him, didn't you?"

He was shaking his head, then tapped something in his ear before calling in the incident and requesting back up for collection of the vampire.

A wave of dizziness flared through my head, and I used the wall at my back to hold myself upright. The whole time, I couldn't stop staring at the sharpness of the angles on Keon's face. His eyes were such a deep green, they looked like a meadow after a storm. Add to that, a touch of something hiding behind his gaze I couldn't decipher.

When he turned his attention completely toward me, offering me a cocky grin, I stiffened. I refused to let him see the impact he had on me. I huffed and blew an upward breath to send the bangs off my brow into a flutter. I put just enough frustration in my action to appear bored and unimpressed by his presence. In truth, I wished the world would crack open and swallow me whole, so I could just run away and hide.

The things I'd let him do to me in the stairwell had fire climbing up my neck. "Well, I better be off then." Evidently, I wouldn't be making it to the library today.

I couldn't move fast enough when the world started to tilt around me. On the inside, I was a complete mess of bad luck and decisions. But I'd been taught early on the importance of concealing my real emotions, so I schooled my face.

"You're bleeding," he said before I could get more than a few steps away.

"I'll be fine." I brushed it off, then looked down at my arms where rivulets of blood rolled down to my fingertips from where my attacker scraped his claws down my arms. Shit!

My head whirred, the motion sending me into a tumble toward the wall.

Strong arms looped around my waist and drew me back. "I got you." Keon pressed my back flush against his solid chest. "You're not going anywhere," he whispered in my ear, his breath dancing on my cheek.

My insides were melting from being so close to him.

"You keep saving me," I murmured, my head blurry

and thoughts a jumbled mess, but I wriggled out of his embrace. "That's three times now."

Next thing I knew, he whisked me into his arms and cradled me against his chest. The whole hall twirled, and I clasped onto his tailored uniform jacket to make my head stop moving.

"Everything's spinning," I murmured.

"I'm going to say you hit your head and lost quite a bit of blood," he explained.

He walked with me in his arms down the hall, just as two guards stormed past us and toward the vampire.

"Three times, hey?" Keon repeated. "I only counted two."

Thinking straight was close to impossible with the lightheaded sensation settling over me. I pressed myself closer to Keon, his arms tight around me, not letting me go. On the way out of the hallway, I closed my eyes and tried to settle my pounding heart. With each inhale, I just breathed in his masculine and woodsy scent. Its familiarity calmed me. As strange as it sounded, his presence offered me something I missed terribly. A connection to the outside world. A reminder I wasn't one of the monsters here. Someone to just hold onto and pretend everything would somehow be alright.

"At the bar," I finally answered his earlier question. "The third time you saved me was at the bar."

"Ah, yes, with that older man hitting on you."

That wasn't what I had meant, but I just let him

believe it. Thoughts were too tangled in my mind to explain anything right then.

We traveled in silence for a long while, and I let myself soften against him, pretending I wasn't in prison.

"We're here, my little shadow," he finally whispered.

I opened my eyes to find we stood in a place I didn't recognize. White walls, no prison cells. Just a wooden door in front of us and behind us was what looked like a doctor's waiting room. Chairs against the walls and a small table with magazines. No windows. Only then did I notice all the furniture was bolted to the tiled floor to avoid being thrown around.

"Where are we?"

He lowered me to my feet, but still held onto my shoulders. His grasp was secure and strong, and most of all, caring. Who was this man? When I glanced up into his spectacular green eyes, all I could think of was that if I was his shadow, he had become my sunshine. I almost cringed out loud at my own dorky thoughts. I clearly hit my head hard.

"You're here to see the prison medic to make sure you're not seriously hurt."

"I've bloodied your uniform." I gestured to the red stains on his shirt from the cuts on my arms.

"I've had worse." He tried to hide his smile as his gaze slid down my body, but I could still see the amused look in his eyes and knew exactly what he referred to. The blood on his dick from when he took my virginity.

I wanted to die. "Worse?"

He winked sexily. "Dr. Brina is expecting you." Keon walked backward before turning and heading out of the waiting room, leaving me completely alone.

I was never going to be able to forget our moment in the bar. He'd remind me with every small thing he did and said... I could see that now. I sucked in a breath. I ought to be angry, but I couldn't stop thinking about his mouth on me. Maybe I was weak, or maybe I had hit my head so hard, I just wasn't thinking straight.

I swallowed hard and faced the door before raising my hand to knock. Except, the door opened abruptly, and I gasped with shock.

CHAPTER 9

KEON

*S*elena.

She was at Nightmare Penitentiary. I'd never seen that coming. From the first night I'd seen her across the courtyard as she somberly strode into the prison with that asshole of a vampire, I'd kept my eye on her. Unable to go more than a few hours without checking in to make sure she was safe.

She'd swept into my world that night at the bar, offered herself to me, and I took everything she was willing to give to me. I was a wolf in sheep's clothing, searching for my meal. And she floated right into my arms like an angel willingly.

I liked to chase my girls, follow them, uncover everything about them before I made my move and claimed what I wanted. But not Selena. She did something to me that night. Saw me as something more than a predator.

That lost girl came looking for escape, for the right man to be her first. Underneath, lay a scared girl, still, she wore her bravery like armor.

It had been fate for her to choose me of all the people in that bar. Any guy would have taken what she gave and walked away unaffected.

But not me.

I had a little problem...I tended to get obsessed. And no girl had stoked my obsession more than her.

And now the girl that starred in all of my day...and night dreams...she'd returned to my life. If I thought my heart was ripped apart after our one night together, then those pieces had just shattered even more.

What she gave me had never left my mind. I still had her underwear, it allowed me to never forget her intoxicating scent. She plagued my thoughts. Her taste and smell remained caught in my mind. Those moans tearing from her throat still did me in. How fucking tight she had been. The swell of her breasts. The lush slick of her pussy.

Fuck. Even just thinking of it now had me hard.

I still pictured myself kneeling behind her as she bent over while shivering with uncertainty. That sweet ass of hers in the air, offering me everything she had. That curvy little body was perfect for me. She was all mine as I sank into her. I knew then that one time would never be enough. And I wouldn't be content until I had her again and again. To drown in her arousing scent. Trace kisses over her neck, the hollow between her breasts, licking up the inside of her thighs.

My groin tightened even more in my pants.

I needed her.

Craved her.

I'd lost my fucking mind.

The thing was, even if she hadn't come to me, I intended to claim her from the moment I saw her step into the bar.

But then, she changed the game on me.

I'd admit, I had my fair share of girls approaching me, but they were never fun. I liked the chase, to dominate my catch, to ignite a hunger in them that they never knew existed.

The harder they fought, the harder I bit back.

That was until Selena.

Please don't stop. Her words undid me… I could see that now. That was the exact moment I broke and forgot all my rules about never falling for anyone.

My heart raced with the memory of finding my little shadow beneath that filth of a vampire daring to touch her. I seethed with the urge to rip his spine out. The fucker was lucky the prison didn't allow me to kill very often, or he'd be plastered to the walls right now in a dozen body parts.

This girl had me messed up.

I waited for the security clearance to open the door from this wing. When the buzz sounded, I palmed open the door and marched back toward the main compound, my thoughts on fire.

How the hell was I going to last having to watch her every day, when all I wanted was to steal her from the world and lock her up all for myself?

SELENA

"You haven't been bitten." Dr. Brina ripped the latex gloves off her hands and swiveled in her seat to dump them into a trash can near her small wooden desk. An oversized painting sat on the wall behind her desk of *Dante's Inferno*. A journey of Dante through Hell depicting how various types of sin would have different consequences in the afterlife. Maybe he'd been onto something considering I'd heard rumors Nightmare Penitentiary was pretty close to Hell.

The metal legs of my chair scraped the tiled floor as I pushed back from the doctor who spun back toward me enthusiastically. She rolled her seat closer to mine. Our knees touched, and she spread her legs to draw me closer, her hands on my thighs. The intensity of her stare left me uneasy.

Most doctors I'd encountered weren't this touchy feely or insisted on being in my personal space.

Dr. Brina on the other hand sat in front of me in a

white doctor's coat. Underneath she wore black leather pants and a matching tank top. Hair as red as fresh blood flowed over one shoulder, drawn into a ponytail. Up closer, she had these green / blue eyes that seemed to change depending on how the light hit them. A deep scar ran over one eye like someone had slashed a blade down her face. As hard as I tried, I couldn't look away, picturing her mauled by a patient at this prison. Just as I had been by the blood-crazed vampire in the hallway.

She pouted her rosy red lips, the color glossy and glinting beneath the fluorescent lights. "You pull away as if I might hurt you. You don't need to fear me, Selena. I am the one that will put you back together should you need it." Her fingers dug into my thighs.

I squirmed on the inside. The way she spoke with a grin on her lips told me she would love such an opportunity. I preferred to never get into that situation. She had seemed to take too much delight in cleaning the blood off my arms, making it uncomfortable enough. Especially with me still sitting here in only my bra and my jumpsuit rolled down to my waist.

I was pretty sure I'd seen her out of the corner of my eye actually taste my blood.

Dr. Brina was a little terrifying.

"How are you feeling?" she asked, so close all I could inhale was a faint floral fragrance, heightened with vanilla notes, and I recognized it at once. Chance Chanel. My mother wore the same perfume. I didn't want to be reminded of my mother considering she'd know where I was and hadn't done anything to try and save me. The smell reminded me how little control sirens had over our lives.

I averted the doctor's gaze and glanced down to my arms, the wounds cleaned and covered with a patchwork of small bandages. The skin blushed red around them, but I'd live. I healed fast.

"The cuts aren't stinging anymore. But my head still feels fuzzy," I answered.

She jutted up to her feet in a flash and crossed her small surgery room. Against the back wall stood a glass cabinet filled with shelves of small plastic containers. She unlocked the small door with a key on the chain around her neck, then grabbed a small bottle and shook it up. "Drink this and the dizziness will stop." She returned and placed the remedy into my hand. Her fingers brushed mine, leaving behind a strange tingle like I'd just touched static. She stared at me with intensity, her head tilting as she watched me. Something about her screamed predator.

I studied the bottle filled with a purplish liquid inside. There were no labels with details on what lay inside.

"It's just a small something I made to help the body heal quickly from blood loss," she explained, her grin widening like a Cheshire cat.

"Guess it's a common thing here." I half laughed

with nerves and twisted the cap until it snapped open and lifted it to my lips. It smelled of blackcurrants, so I drank it back in one go. She was the doctor and I had to assume she wouldn't give me something to make me sicker. A strange taste lingered on the back of my tongue afterward.

Up on her feet abruptly, Dr. Brina stormed across the room in a few quick steps and wrenched open the door. "Alright, Selena. You might feel a bit groggy for a day or so, but you are fine to go." Her voice was suddenly curt and impatient. "I should mention, you will also be booked into counseling with the prison psychiatrist as part of the rehabilitation program of the prison."

I threw the empty container into the trash can and pulled the jumpsuit crumpled down to my waist up my body. I threaded my arms through the sleeves and quickly buttoned it up. She didn't even wait for me to dress before opening the door. Luckily no one stood outside the room or they would have gotten an eyeful. I made my way toward her.

Dr. Brina gripped her waist, her toe tapping the floor. Gone was the curiosity in her gaze, along with the woman who seemed to enjoy being in my space. She now glared at me as if she might sprout horns if I didn't leave her office fast enough.

The air felt thick and that earlier tenderness vanished, replaced by the new person who couldn't wait to get rid of me.

I headed outside and turned to thank her, but the door shut in my face.

Wow. Someone was a crazy psycho. Turning back around I found a guard, leaning a shoulder into the wall, arms folded over his chest, waiting for me. His hood was pulled back and I could see that he had short sandy colored hair, his mouth twisted into a wry frown. I ought to be glad it wasn't Keon, yet a tingling sensation in my gut surfaced. Okay, I'd admit it. I was disappointed it hadn't been Keon waiting for me.

* * *

The delicious aroma of pancakes woke my senses, calling to me, enticing my stomach. I salivated as I opened my eyes. While light poured out of my open doorway, chasing the darkness in my cell away. Someone had left the door open and by the silence around me, everyone must still be sleeping.

Pushing myself to my feet, I climbed out of bed and glanced out into the hallway where I spotted a wheeled tray with a plate piled high with pancakes.

I shuddered on my feet, utterly bewildered and torn. On one hand, this was the epitome of a horror movie. I was tempted by fluffy pancakes sitting just out of my cell. But then again, pancakes!

My betraying stomach growled and I stepped forward, figuring I could just look outside. The moment I spotted something creepy like a clown, I was going to run.

Creeping closer, I stuck my head out and looked left and right. Empty. Not a soul in sight down the hallway. All the other prison doors were shut and not a sound came from any of them, which was strange in itself. I had become used to the screams and moans of my fellow inmates. It was like white noise at this point.

I refocused on the pancakes and my mouth salivated. In truth, I hadn't eaten many pancakes in my life for the simple reason that I'd been prohibited from doing so. I had tried them a couple of times at school, but she somehow always knew when I did. Then I'd receive the lecture of how bad processed food was for me, how I'd put on weight. And my daily workout would go from one hour...to three.

Right now though, the pancakes called to me.

If some fool left them out here as they made a delivery somewhere, they were free for the taking, right? Their loss, my gain.

Quick steps took me closer and I grabbed a piece. It was lathered in maple syrup, so I rolled the pancake into a cigar shape and took a huge bite.

I moaned. Holy shit this was the best tasting thing in the world! It melted on my tongue, the sweetness addictive. I finished the rest in two bites, then reached for another piece when someone cleared their throat behind me.

I froze on the spot, my hand still outstretched.

"Selena," the female voice said with accusation, reminding me too much of my mother.

Turning around, I found Dr. Brina walking toward me from down the hallway. Her black stilettos click clacked on the concrete floor as she sauntered closer in her black leather pants and cropped tank top. A sliver of creamy white flesh peeked out from under her top with each step. Crimson long hair fluttered over her shoulders. Anywhere else and I would be mesmerized by her. She was so beautiful, I would have thought she was a vampire at first glance. Except, I'd been close enough to know she was something I couldn't work out. A supernatural being that left me baffled.

"You are predictable," she accused, her gaze drifting from me to the plate of food.

I stiffened. "I'm pretty sure everyone loves pancakes."

Her eyes narrowed as if challenging my response.

"Wait!" The cogs in my head were spinning. "It was you who put them outside my cell and opened the door, wasn't it? Why?"

"Because I could tell you've been deprived the simple joys of life. You're too thin and haven't been eating. And like you just said, not many can resist freshly cooked pancakes."

"Is this a test?" I find myself licking my sticky fingers, unable to stop myself, the maple syrup delicious.

Dr. Brina shrugged as she glided closer, swinging her hips in a seductive walk.

I stepped backward from her approach. That intensity in her eyes returning.

"Be a good girl, Selena."

Those words rang like warning bells in my head, blaring for me to run out of there. I let out a breath, feeling like I'd just walked into a trap. Still something didn't make sense.

Why lure me out here where there were cameras? And most importantly, what did she want?

Her lips turned up in the corners as I recoiled. But she was near me in a flash like she'd moved at the speed of light. My whole body went rigid at how close she stood.

The hairs on my nape raised.

"Don't be afraid," she cooed, the sound strangely comforting and soothing.

I wanted to run, but my feet wouldn't respond.

"I like my meals sweet," she whispered. "And not afraid. Fear gives it such a bitter taste."

"What do you mean?" Why was it so hard to think straight, to remember why I even stood out here.

"Selena," Dr. Brina said. "Just breathe and forget everything else."

As if my body now obeyed her orders, my muscles softened and the fogginess in my head thickened.

"Selena," she repeated. "Focus on me."

My heartbeat was pounding through my veins, and I knew I'd forgotten something. What I had to remember sat on the forefront of my mind just out of reach.

"You're so stunning, so special." Dr. Brina pushed a loose strand of hair behind my ear, her touch leaving behind a trail of tingles.

I lifted my gaze to meet hers. She was gorgeous, so irresistible, still a chill ran down my spine despite the heat from her finger trailing across my neck.

Instinctively, I backed up. I'd always found women beautiful and sexy, but I wasn't attracted to them, not the way I was to men. Yet, with the way Dr. Brina stared at me, I felt her intentions, felt the sizzling fire she emitted.

She reached out to touch my arm. Even through my bandages, the fire of her hand bled into me.

Dr. Brina brushed my hair over my shoulder and traced the back of her fingers down the curve of my neck. In her heels, she stood taller than me. In all honesty I wasn't sure how to feel. Still, my body trembled.

She released a deep breath, and smiled widely.

"I'm not really into this," I admitted.

With a simple shake of her head, she dismissed me. "It's not what you think," she whispered in my ear.

Our bodies pressed closer, chest to chest. My breaths raced, and I wanted to move away, to push her off me, but it felt as though my body no longer responded to me.

"Please," I begged while she laughed in response.

I gasped as her teeth scraped gently against my neck. My heart pounded in my chest so hard I was convinced it would burst free.

Teeth tore into my neck, and I screamed, my body deflating in her arms.

I woke up just then on my cot, shaking and terrified...and tired, like my energy had leaked out during the night. Taking a quick glance at the door to my cell I saw that it was firmly shut and there was no mysterious tray of breakfast food waiting outside to tempt me.

What the fuck had been in that purple drink Dr. Brina had given me?

I didn't think I would be making any more trips to the medical wing in the future. I had a feeling that Dr. Brina was a lot more dangerous than most of the injuries I would face.

CHAPTER 10

Another day had gone by, and I thankfully had no more crazy dreams about Dr. Brina. I blamed whatever she gave me to drink for the delusional nightmare and tried not to think about her very much.

Now, I was once again washing dishes, chatting idly with one of the cooks who I had a sneaking suspicion was a shifter based on the long tongue that I had seen flop out of her mouth when she thought I wasn't looking.

I was scrubbing a pan with a particularly difficult crusty residue when I asked the cook a question about if they made food for the Warden, and if so, what his favorite food was.

My question was met with silence.

Unsure if I asked a question they weren't allowed to answer, I turned my head to look at her.

She was gone.

Feeling uneasy since the food she was cooking was still sitting there on the stove, threatening to bubble over, I looked around to see where she had gone.

And I saw him.

The prisoner from the other day. The one who had practically made my underwear combust just by being near his presence.

I was frozen in place with a strange mixture of lust and fear. After all...this prisoner may be hot, but he was also in the maximum security section for a reason.

How did he get out of his cell? I thought that this place was supposedly unescapable.

I was going to die.

I should have known better than to meet eyes with a probable psychopath.

I began to back away, not taking my eyes off of him. He just stared at me, his eyes devouring every inch of me until I felt like I was melting.

His mouth slowly moved into a smirk.

"How did you get out?" I finally choked when I backed up as far as I could go in the room.

"I have my ways," he rumbled softly. I swear, I could hear the smile in his voice, and it did nothing to relieve the hormonal war going on inside me. That voice was going to be featuring in my fantasies for a long time to come if I survived this encounter. Deep, masculine, and raspy- it pulsed straight to my core.

"Why wouldn't you just leave then? Why would you

come to find me?" I asked, fear rapidly building inside of me as he continued to move towards me. The way he was stalking me reminded me of a panther. "I warn you, I probably don't taste good," I add lamely, grabbing a wooden spoon and holding it out in front of me like a weapon.

He just smirked at me and continued to prowl towards me.

"You're all I've thought about since you came by my cell. And I'm not in the habit of withholding pleasure from myself," he said calmly as he continued to move.

"You're crazy," I murmured, setting the spoon down and grabbing a metal spatula from the counter that at least had a sharp edge.

"What's your name, little one?" he asked, unperturbed by the fear I was exuding or the weapon I brandished.

Like I was going to tell him that. I pursed my lips stubbornly and he laughed, a soft throaty chuckle that threatened to set my skin on fire with its deliciousness.

"I'd like to know your name before I fuck you, but I'll do without if I have to," he murmured. "I'm Alaric."

My mouth opened in shock, and then I blinked and he was in front of me. I took a deep breath in shock and couldn't help but savor his smell, a combination of some kind of exotic musk and oddly enough...the ocean. He stood there, inches from my face, studying me closely, his expression impassive, the heat in his steely grey eyes momentarily captivating me.

I blinked, trying to shake myself from whatever spell he had weaved on me. I was about to tell him off, or actually try screaming for help. But he shocked me by leaning in slowly, his soft lips just barely grazing mine, once, twice, then closing over mine in a supple kiss. His hot, wet tongue slid into my mouth, tasting me, exploring.

I should have fought it, but when he pushed his tongue past my parted lips with a languid sweep and a low groan...it seemed to reverberate straight through me clear down to my soul.

Somehow I knew a kiss with him would feel like this. Warm, slow, indulgent. The pleasure was almost jarring, like the first shock of sticky sweet caramel on my tongue, tasting so good my mind couldn't quite comprehend it. But I opened my mouth for more, completely a glutton for the forbidden decadence. He fucked my mouth with his tongue, deep, long licks that resonated down to my core.

He lifted me up onto the counter and I didn't even care about how unsanitary it was for me to be sitting where the prison food was prepared. Surely they had magic for that...

Alaric wrapped his hands in my long hair and I arched into him instinctively, silently begging for more, and something about the action changed every-thing. Little pulses of desire shimmered through my entire body, and I could actually feel my clit pulsing. The kiss went from slow and languid to rough and desperate between one heartbeat and the next. When his tongue thrust past my lips this time, it was harder somehow, more primitive. He tightened his fingers in my hair, holding me there as he nipped at my bottom lip. I opened wider, taking everything he wanted to give me. We were moaning and panting into each other's mouths whenever we parted for air. The quiver of need between us was so violent, it became a physical manifestation, and both our hands shook.

When Alaric pushed his hips against me, I could feel the hard outline of his cock through his prison uniform. I fisted his shirt, stretched out the neckline as I gasped, and my entire body clenched from the rush of knowing he was aching too.

"Oh, I need—" I tossed my head backwards in beautiful agony. He responded by leaning down and sucking on the soft spot at the curve of my neck, making me jerk when the pleasure of it found a direct line to my clit. I couldn't even begin to verbalize my desperation, but I tried.

"Please, Alaric. I—" I choked when he pulled up the top of my uniform, not hesitating to take it all the way off. I had a brief moment where I once again wondered what in the hell I was doing.

But then Alaric groaned as he looked over my body, and the sound of it sent heat burning from my face down to my neck and chest.

"Fuck, you blush all over." He ran his thumb down the valley between my breasts, his fingers grazing the edge of my right one. "That's sexy as shit. Your skin's just so fucking smooth. Like, flawless. No tan lines, and look how you get all flushed just from me looking at you."

He cupped my left breast with his other hand and grunted, his stomach muscles clenching noticeably. "I have a thing about women blushing."

"Y-you do?" I wanted to turn my head and hide my embarrassment, but it was captivating to watch the way Alaric stared down at my body. It felt a bit like seeing a car accident—a part of me wanted to look away, but I couldn't.

"You're fucking perfect," he breathed softly. He couldn't seem to look away from my breasts. He rubbed a thumb over my nipple through the thin bra that had come with my uniform and provided almost no support whatsoever.

He suddenly flicked the back of my bra open, in a move so smooth that I didn't want to think about how many women it had taken to make him that way. Once my bra slid off my arms, he circled the tip of my breast reverently, making me moan and arch into him again. Screw embarrassment, my eyes closed because that felt wonderful.

"I wonder what you'll look like after you come."

"What?" I squeaked as his thumb continued to trace little circles over my nipple that was tight from the pleasure of it.

Alaric wrapped his arms around my back, forcing

me to arch into him. He leaned down, sucking my nipple into his mouth. Holy hell. It felt so good. I got weak-kneed, my body giving out and wanting to slide off the counter, down to the ground.

He held me up before I could fall. I felt his biceps clench under my fingers as I clung to him like a lifeline. He pulled me closer and moved his lips back up to my neck. My breasts would have mourned the loss, but I was already in sensory overload. Everything felt good. We were both breathless, and when he reached up, tugging my hair, exposing the curve of my neck, I arched into the tight hold, giving myself over to it like an addict as he sucked and licked the line of my throat up to the tender spot behind my ear.

"I'm gonna eat you out until you scream, baby."

I wasn't paying much attention. His promise was lost until he slipped his free hand to my waist and began to pull on the drawstring of my loose uniform pants.

Once my pants were undone, his hand slid under the lining of my underwear, touching me expertly. My face flamed because I was so very wet, swollen, and aching.

"Baby." He groaned, pushing a finger into me without invitation or warning. I gasped and jerked from the white-hot rush of pleasure as he breathed into my ear. "Oh, yeah, that's going to be mine."

Oh.

No way. What was I doing?

I should have shoved Alaric off of me, but I was having trouble thinking because everything he was doing felt so good.

It was like he had drugged me. I couldn't stop him. I couldn't explain anything. Instead I threw my head back, shaking and needy as he moved down once more. Sucking on my nipples again. Licking my skin as if I was the best thing he'd ever tasted. Lower against my stomach, and then he was there.

I had given up on willing my body to stop. I helped him pull off the standard grey underwear they made us wear. I didn't worry about anything, especially not the fact that I was completely exposed to a man I barely knew but felt this crazy connection with.

He groaned his appreciation as he looked me over, deep and guttural. The sound was so erotic, my core tightened and my nipples hardened, goose bumps rising along my skin despite the building heat between our bodies. He held me close.

"I love your body," he said gruffly against my skin as his grip tightened on my hip. While he continued to taste me, his hands continued to move, gliding down my skin, my side, my waist. He made a hungry noise as he slowly explored every inch of my body down to my thighs. "Curves in all the right places." His voice sounded like sex, like primal, raw sex. His eyes glowed like silver orbs in the dim lighting of the kitchen as he lifted his head up to look at me. "So pretty, baby."

Something caught in my chest, because the way he

was looking at me was so genuine. His look was too much for what this was. Nothing.

Alaric stood up to tug at the back of his shirt. He pulled it off in one fluid motion and then tossed it aside. I studied him, now bare-chested, showing off a few tattoos. Everything inside me stopped. Holy hell. He looked unreal with flawless, lean flesh over hard, rippling muscle. His body probably put everyone to shame. His stomach, chest, traps, and arms were powerful, heavy slabs of muscle, built to perfection. He had a defined eight-pack and that sexy V running along his hips disappearing into his low-slung pants. I wanted to run my tongue along that V. Worship it. Worship him. His chest and stomach were smooth, showing every nuance of his sculpted chest and defined abs. He was the embodiment of my every fantasy come to life, everything I had ever desired in a man. And more. I idly wondered how much time prisoners here were allowed to spend in the gym for him to look like that.

"You are perfect," I said, mesmerized.

In that moment I forgot about everything but this beautiful, dangerous man in front of me. What the hell was I even worried about? He picked me up and walked over to the wall, pushing me against it as he continued to hold my weight like I weighed nothing.

"I need you," I begged. He sucked in a sharp breath, eyeing me in surprise and a little smugness at the desperation in my voice.

"Yeah?"

"Yes."

Alaric didn't hesitate. He leaned down and sucked on one taut nipple again, making me moan and arch my back against the wall. I threaded my fingers into his silky hair, holding him to me as he continued to kiss me all over. His bare skin felt amazing against mine. So incredibly intimate in a way I hadn't expected.

I watched the emotions play over his handsome face as he licked and teased me. A fresh sheen of sweat coated my body, making the slide of skin against skin slick. My legs were parted to support his hard, muscular form in between them. He pushed his rough palm against my knees, and I opened up wider for him.

An involuntary moan escaped my throat as his gentle kneading he had been doing turned rougher. I heard a hungry noise rumbling out of him, and then his lips, tongue, and teeth were exploring my quickly heating flesh with a new urgency. His greedy hands on my thighs turned desperate, moving higher, seeking more skin as his hard cock rubbed against me.

"Fuck. You know you're mine… You know you were made for me." He sounded equally aroused and frustrated.

Like a man born to recklessly take what pleasures life offered him, Alaric ran a thumb down my folds, still holding me up with his other arm.

"I have to taste this again," he said gruffly.

There wasn't an ounce of hesitance or insecurity in him, not with this, not stripped bare and staring at me like he wanted to remember all this as badly as I did. Then he gently lowered me and got down on his knees, hooking one of my legs over his shoulder. I watched, mesmerized by the sheer boldness in him as he sucked on my clit as if he owned it. The pleasure was blinding. I couldn't help but close my eyes against it. My fingers tightened in his hair of their own accord, and for just a moment, I was worried it was too much. Then he pushed one finger into me, doubling the surge of bliss, and I couldn't fight it anyway. I didn't want to.

I cried out his name when his touch curved upward, hitting something inside me that made the feel of his tongue against my clit that much more potent. It was overwhelming, but I let myself sink into the rapture of it simply because I had no idea how to stop myself.

"Alaric!" My legs were shaking as the coil of pleasure tightened too fast to control. I pitched against his face, pulling his hair and opening wide to the onslaught when the ecstasy slammed into me hard, taking my breath away.

"What's your name," he asked stopping right before I went over the edge.

"Bastard," I cried out.

"Your name," he ordered."

"Selena," I breathed as he immediately went back to work.

"Yes, Yes, Yes," I chanted breathlessly as wave after

wave of pleasure crashed over me. My entire body quivered from it. My insides clenched to the hard, fast rhythm of release, and he rubbed against that soft spot over and over in response to the unspoken plea. I squeezed my eyes shut tighter when I felt myself coming again.

He was magic. He had to be.

I bit my lip, choking on my cries. My body was betraying me completely though. Alaric could feel how strong my orgasm was, inside and out. It hadn't even fully waned before I became far too sensitive for his mouth, and I tugged at his hair.

He surprised me by pulling away, but he was still stroking me with his fingers. Somewhere along the way, he had worked a second one in, and it felt amazing. Alaric was over me now, watching me as he fucked me with his fingers. It dragged out my second release for what felt like forever, making me bite my lip even harder.

He stopped touching me only to reach up and free my bottom lip. His fingers left the tang of me on my lip and I inhaled quickly when he leaned down and licked it away a second later.

"No hiding." He breathed against my lips. "I like hearing it."

I blinked, stunned by how much that turned me on. "O-okay," I stuttered.

My body was still raw and tingling from two powerful orgasms. When he reached down and pushed a finger back into me again, I gasped at the onslaught.

"You're tight, baby." Alaric stroked me again to prove his point, making me clench around him.

I wasn't about to tell this sex god that this was only the second time that I'd had sex. I squeezed my eyes shut tighter

"Has it been awhile?" Alaric sounded amused at the thought. Maybe he was thinking I had been in the prison for awhile.

He had a little bit of an accent the more turned on he got and it only served to fuel the flame raging inside me, especially when he reached down and grabbed my right hand, pushed it against the front of his pants, forcing me to feel the long, thick outline of him.

"I'm not going to be able to keep myself away," he growled.

I cupped him on instinct at the thought of doing this with him again, watching the way his eyes grew heavy-lidded from my touch.

With a boldness that I didn't know I possessed, I pulled at the tie holding up his uniform bottoms and then slowly pulled them down . Alaric flattened both hands against the wall, supporting his upper body weight, and then dropped his head to watch me free him.

"Fuck," he groaned when I stroked the length of him.

"Fuck is right," I murmured, a little bit distracted

because I couldn't believe how thick he was in my hand. I was stuck halfway between being nervous and so turned on I couldn't look away from the sight of my hand around him. I stroked him from root to tip, and then rubbed my thumb over the head of it, practically salivating over what it would feel like pushing inside me.

"See something you like?"

I blinked up at him. "What?"

He smiled a cruel smile and grunted and arched into the embrace of my hand. "I'm going to ruin you," he growled as he continued to thrust in my hand.

I watched the way my hand moved down the thick, tanned length of his cock, feeling breathless again.

He suddenly stilled my hand and pulled away from me briefly before hoisting me up in his arms once again. I wrapped my legs around him, because I needed him in me, even if it was going to be a tight fit. We were skin to skin at last. Words were gone as quickly as they'd showed up, replaced with a surge of emotion I wasn't expecting. I caressed his face as he pushed close to me.

The fire in his grey eyes nearly consumed me as Alaric studied me.

"Selena-" His voice was a little choked. "I—"

I placed my fingers over his lips before he could finish. I could sense some sort of confession in his voice, and it was too much. I couldn't hear it. Not when we were both locked away in this hell. It was crazy and insane and made about as much sense as any of the rest of it did, but I didn't want to know what he was going to say, and I cut him off at the pass.

"Just give me what I want," I pleaded, because I needed it desperately.

He groaned in defeat and buried his face in the curve of my neck. His lips felt like heaven, making a fresh sheen of pleasure dance over my skin. I turned my head, giving him better access as I traced the muscles of his back and let him work one hand between our naked bodies. I could feel his cock, hard and ready against my stomach, but he touched me instead. The seduction felt slow as he teased me and stretched me and made me so wet and needy I no longer cared how big he was.

I was shifting and moaning against him, pushing myself up against his hand. If he didn't do this soon, I was going to come again. It had already been three times and he hadn't even fucked me yet.

I gasped when he rubbed his thumb against my clit and begged again, "Please."

He stopped touching me and pushed his other hand into my hair, tugging it pointedly and looking down at me again. "I like to watch. I wanna see your face when I take you."

I closed my eyes, feeling exposed and all the more turned on because of it. "Okay." He shifted, and I arched against him when I felt him against my opening, pushing forward in a slow, indulgent claiming. When the broad tip of his cock breached me, my mouth fell open with a gasp.

Goose bumps spread over my skin, the pleasure was deeper than before, more potent, and I dug my nails into his shoulders when it started to overwhelm me. The pain only seemed to spur him on.I tried to bite my bottom lip to keep myself quiet as he rocked in and out of me, but he growled, "No, let me hear it. Let me hear all of it."

He took me the rest of the way in one hard thrust that made me cry out from the surge of ecstasy. "That's it, baby. Let everyone in this hell hole hear you get off on me fucking you."

I gasped at his harsh words. He buried his face against my neck again, and then bit hard enough to leave a mark. The next time he spoke, it was in a different language, but the words were just as harsh and jagged, breathless and defiantly sexual in a way that was easy to understand, even if I couldn't understand it. He pulled out and took me again before I could catch my breath.

Heavenly Goddess, the friction was incredible. I found myself clinging to him as he took me hard, over and over again, making the pleasure build and build until I was dragging my nails down his back and coming before either of us expected it. He rode out the storm with me, thrusting harder, extending the wild rush of ecstasy so long I was winded and sweaty when it started to wane. Alaric was still moving, and I realized he hadn't climaxed with me. His voice was ragged as he made those low, masculine grunts of pleasure against the curve of my neck with every thrust. When he did speak, it was still in that other, mystical sounding language, whispered against my ear like the confessions of a dying man.

I could feel the tension in him, in the muscles flexing under my fingers and the way everything about him seemed coiled tight, like a snake about to strike. That seemed unfair, and I ran my hands up to his hair. I fisted it and lifted his head to claim his lips in a wild, openmouthed kiss. He pushed his tongue past my lips as he started moving faster, harder. Somehow, one of my knees had become hooked under his arm, leaving me completely open to the thrust of his hips against mine. We were sweaty and sticky, but none of it mattered as he kissed me again and then slipped a hand between our straining bodies, finding my clit, making me aware of how wet I was, forcing me to feel what a messy, sticky business sex with Alaric was, and I loved it. So much so I moaned into our next kiss and just let him have his way with me.

"I don't think I can," I moaned. But even as I said it, I felt it building again. I didn't think I would be able to walk tomorrow, but I was going to come again.

"Solaris renta," Alaric moaned in my ear. He punctuated the strange words by tugging on my hair again and finally growled something against my ear that I understood, "Now!"

I screamed when another orgasm ripped through my body, followed by another and another. They rolled together in a neverending tide and I was only faintly aware of my screams as the pleasure threatened to black me out.

What had he done to me?

He gripped my ass, holding me tightly against him as he fucked me harder, broken phrases bursting out of him as my orgasms continued to wash over me.

My orgasms continued until after he came with a loud, feral shout that echoed throughout the room. Only then did whatever he had done to me fade away. I continued to whimper as the last vestiges of pleasure coursed through my body. My voice was hoarse from screaming and Alaric was having to hold up my entire weight as I had no strength left.

I started to notice the little things then, like the feel of his sweaty skin against mine and the fact that we were still in the bloody kitchen and I had just let this stranger fuck me against a wall.

He was leaning against me, pushing me against the wall, and his weight was almost too much. I was so tired though I could barely think to complain. Instead I hugged him tighter, completely wrapping myself around him.

As I continued to come back down to reality, what I had done and where I was began to beat through my head. Had I really just done that?

And what the hell was he that he had made me come like that again and again?

I struggled to push him away and he reluctantly allowed space between us.

"What are you?" I asked hoarsely, glaring at him and feeling somehow betrayed as I came to the stark realization now that I was in control of my body that he had used magic on me.

A smug grin curled up his face. "Do you think just any creature could do that to you, Selena?" he gloated.

The sick feeling inside of me grew larger, pushing out the orgasmic afterglow I had been feeling. I struggled to push him away even more.

"Get off me," I growled, and he threw his head back and laughed, the sound stupidly attractive. Everything about him was attractive and I was furious at my body for betraying me over and over again when it came to this beautiful creature.

"You mean you haven't heard the rumors about me while out on your food runs?" he asked, stepping away, unabashed about his nudity. "I would think my reputation would proceed me."

Suddenly it hit me what he was. It should have been obvious. Incubi were similar to sirens in their ability to attract...but sirens didn't feed on sexual energy.

"Did you just feed on me?" I gasped, horrified as I picked up my clothes and began to hurry and pull them on.

"Do you really think the slop they feed me would

keep this going?" he asked, gesturing to his perfect, still naked body.

I groaned and rubbed a hand down my face, cursing myself a thousand times over. There were way too many parasites in this prison.

Taking a deep breath, I resumed glaring at him. "Get away from me and leave right now or I'll scream," I threatened.

He stepped closer to me again. "Done so soon? I was really thinking we should do another round."

Fury swept through me. I opened my mouth and began to scream...quite loudly. Fun fact about sirens, we had excellent lung capacities, and anyone in the near vicinity would hear me, and hopefully come.

"What the fuck?" he growled, pushing away from me and backing up with an annoyed look on his face. "Can you shut up," he yelled as I began to scream louder. The sound was enough that it forced him to cover his ears before I burst his eardrum.

"I'm leaving," he barked before grabbing his clothes and hastily putting on his pants before darting out of the room.

A few seconds later a pack of guards came streaming into the kitchen on alert for a threat.

But the threat was gone.

He was gone.

And my body already missed him.

Shit.

* * *

*D*espite my behavior, or maybe because of my behavior, I still had another food run to do before I could go back to my cell and wallow in self pity. My guard for the food run was in a pissed off mood, but I was just glad he wasn't Keon. It probably would have been really uncomfortable to see my first lover right after getting pounded against the kitchen wall by an incubus. I'm sure all of the guards knew exactly what happened, the smell of sex was rampant in that room. The food was probably all tainted as well. I kind of felt bad for the prisoners I was about to help feed.

But only kind of.

I was taken the opposite way from my usual routes, and I breathed a sigh of relief that I wouldn't be seeing Alaric right after what had just happened. Which just reminded me about the fact that he'd been able to escape from his cell.

How was that even possible?

Maybe the guards could be bought after all.

The only problem with getting out of your cell was that you still couldn't get out of the prison itself. I hadn't heard of anyone ever escaping before.

Surely Alaric would have left if he knew a way out.

But if he did know a way out...I would do almost anything to get that information.

Tucking that thought process away for later, I

concentrated on not tripping on the suddenly uneven floor.

We'd just walked through a large metal gate into a part of the prison that made the rest of the place seen seem like Beverly Hills. The floor was uneven, covered in rocks and upturned roots where they'd just let nature take its course. The walls were made of black rock as well and they were covered in algae. I could hear the faint drip drip of water as water leaked down from the ceiling. It was dimmer here than in other parts of the prison, and the set up honestly resembled something from a horror film. It was also quieter here, like the prisoners here were so beat down that they didn't have it in them to moan and cry like in the other sections.

There were no cots in the cells here, only a damp floor to sleep on with a hole in the corner where I assumed they did their business. The sight was heartbreaking and made me instantly rethink my stance on my circumstances here.

It could always be worse.

I shakily slid the trays through the slats of the cells. The food I'd been given to pass out looked worse than anything I'd seen. I was pretty sure there was mold on the roll of the last tray and spit in the soup on another. I felt sick just passing it out.

Suddenly a crack ripped through the air followed by an anguished moan. Again and again, the two sounds echoed through the hallways, the moans getting progressively louder as the whipping continued.

I looked in panic at my guard, thinking that surely whoever was being punished wouldn't survive it, but the asshole looked completely nonplussed. He actually looked like he was savoring the anguished cries. I made a mental note that this guard was a bit sadistic, grateful that his hood was down so that I could see his face and remember him later.

I moved faster, feeling a violent urge to see what was going on. I knew there was nothing I could do, but still, I went quicker until the next cell was the one the sounds were coming from.

After dropping off yet another tray of decaying food that the prisoner was probably better off not eating at all, I pushed the cart forward until I could see inside the next cell.

I let out a little squeak when I saw what was going on.

It was the fae from the other night. It was now obvious where he was getting the wounds on his back from.

He was on his knees on the ground, his pale hair hanging down over his face, his arms stretched out in front of him and tied to a metal pole that was sticking out from the wall. Two guards were standing behind him, giant bullwhips in their hands. As I watched, the guards took turns cracking their whips across the fae's back. His back resembled hamburger meat, a bloody mess of broken flesh that brought tears streaming down my face. What could he possibly have done to deserve something like this?

I knew I was expected to keep walking, I obviously wasn't delivering a tray to this cell. He wouldn't be able to eat with his wounds like that even if the food was edible. The only reason that he was still alive at all with how many times they had whipped him was that he was a fae. They probably came the closest to all of the supernaturals of actually being immortal. It was almost impossible for them to be killed.

I had a feeling this fae was probably wishing for death at the moment though. Which begs the question… how did someone like him end up in this prison? What could he have done to land himself a sentence in these pits?

I took a step forward after hearing a grunt from my guard and my cart hit a rock, making the trays clang as I righted the cart.

The fae had just collapsed onto the ground with one of the guards barking at him to get up. As he struggled to his elbows, his head turned and I could see his brilliant blue eyes staring at me. They were cloudy with pain, no hint of recognition in their lovely depths. I was caught in their gaze though. In that moment I felt like his lifeline and I was frozen in place as we continued to stare at each other as the guards continued to rain down their torture.

The cart was suddenly yanked forward, breaking my eye contact with the fae as I struggled not to fall.

"Keep moving," my guard barked, and I once again looked at the fae as I slowly began to push my cart forward. But he lowered his gaze to the ground again.

I continued to look back until he was out of sight. The sounds of his torture followed me for the rest of my time delivering meals that night.

It followed me to my cell after my shift ended.

And it followed me into my dreams after I finally fell asleep.

The sound of his cries and the sight of those lovely, heartbroken eyes.

CHAPTER 11

couldn't get the fae out of my mind. It had been days, and the memory of those eyes were burned into my brain.

I hated it.

I didn't have room in my life to care about the fate of another creature. Not when my own life was so up in the air.

But on the bright side, the fate of the fae at least distracted me from the clusterfuck that seemed to surround me at Nightmare Penitentiary. I was so distracted thinking about him, that I couldn't think about Keon or Alaric.

Not that I didn't see them.

Because I did.

Keon always seemed to be the guard assigned to me lately. He said very little, but I could feel him watching me, always watching, always there. I probably should have been creeped out like a normal person, but I'd never said I was anywhere close to being normal. I relished in the attention, even as I vowed not to repeat our rendezvous. His presence made me feel protected though. I knew as long as he was near me—which he always seemed to be—the monsters that lurked in the cages of the prison wouldn't be able to hurt me.

My behavior in the kitchen with Alaric had alienated me a bit from the others. There was an air of fear laced in all of my interactions with them, like they expected me to sic Alaric on them if they upset me. I still hadn't been able to find out exactly why Alaric was in the maximum security section of the prison...or in prison at all. And it was a bit infuriating. I hadn't heard anything from the others about his incubus powers, which meant that the fear they exuded had nothing to do with that part of him. But it was the part of him that pissed me off the most.

Because of my newly strained relationship with the others in the kitchen, I'd been sent back to the maximum security section of the prison multiple times. And while I enjoyed seeing Sinclair and had been able to sneak her some rock candy as I delivered her food, seeing Alaric was pure torture.

There was always a knowing glance in his eye when I came to his cell, and my body betrayed me every time, leaving me aching and breathless and wanting...

I blamed my body's reaction on the fact that Alaric was an incubus...but I was pretty sure that actually had little to do with what had happened. I had wanted him more than I'd ever wanted anyone else. I still wanted him with a frantic desperation that both shamed me and aroused me at the same time.

Like I said...my life at Nightmare Penitentiary was a clusterfuck of epic proportions.

But I still couldn't forget my fae.

I'd started calling him "my fae" after that night. There was something so tragic about him that it called to me. Like only he could understand the damage that was in my soul, because it was in his soul too.

Realizing that I was thinking about him once again, I stirred the giant pot of chili I'd been helping to prepare a little too vigorously, and it sloshed out the sides, garnering a frustrated sigh from one of the cooks who, before Alaric, probably would have ripped me a new one for wasting food.

I smiled apologetically and got back to work. Still, the image of him stayed with me until I couldn't take not knowing anything about him anymore.

I set down my spoon and turned to the cook who was trying to ignore me. I was pretty sure she was a hag of some sort. I'd seen a spoon moving by itself after she'd pointed to it one time. That, combined with her grizzled appearance suggested I was right. But she was the only option that I had right now.

"There's a fae prisoner here. Have you seen him?" I asked, my voice sounding a bit desperate.

She hummed non-committedly.

"Does that mean you've heard about him or you haven't heard about him?" I pressed, a little annoyed at this point.

I would love to see her resist Alaric if he'd turned his attention to her. I really shouldn't be punished for it.

"I've heard of him," she said in a tone that was meant to broker no more questions.

"It's unusual for a fae to be in a regular supernatural prison...is it not?" I asked.

She humphed again.

I was tempted to push the entire pot of chili over.

She must have finally sensed that I was on the edge, because she picked up my abandoned spoon and pointed at me. "Take it," she croaked. "Keep stirring, and I'll talk."

I quickly grabbed the spoon and began stirring once again, taking extra care not to spill any this time.

"You're right that the fae usually handle their matters themselves, but the rumor is that this fae entered the kingdom and did something so heinous that the fae had no choice but to cast him out of their realm. The Warden apparently assured them that he would subject the exiled fae to an eternity of torture." She paused for dramatic effect just then. "I pity the creature. But it is nice to have such a looker around the prison, isn't it?" she said with a wink.

I tried to ignore that she was taking pleasure from

the fae's plight and continued on. "Do you know what he's accused of doing?" I asked.

Her face scrunched up. "Oh, it isn't that he's accused of it, he was found with the weapon in his hand and the king's blood all over him," she said, enthusiastically waving her spoon around.

"He killed the Light Fae King?" I asked with a gasp, not expecting that. The fae were notoriously reclusive, spending as much time in Fairie away from the rest of the supernatural world as possible, but still...you would have thought that I would have heard about something like that. Or at least, heard Julian discussing it, since he sometimes did trade with the fae. "The fae have a way of looking back into the past to ensure they don't make mistakes. And whatever they did proved that he killed the king," the cook continued.

Another of the workers, a cyclops, piped in just then. I'd been so enthralled in the cook's story that I hadn't noticed her walk into the room. "I've heard that he wasn't just a run of the mill fae," she said, her one eye wide-eyed and unblinking. "He was the eldest of the Light Fae princes. And the king was his father."

The cook cleared her throat. "That's not true. I heard he's an assassin from the Dark Fae Kingdom sent to kill their enemy."

The cyclop shook. Her head, disgruntled.

I stopped stirring, horror-stricken at the story and possible reasons for the fae killing a king. It hadn't been what I was expecting at all. For some reason, I'd created some kind of tragic backstory for the fae where he'd been falsely imprisoned, but I'd also heard about the magic the fae used to see the past. And as far as I'd heard, it was never wrong.

Still, a part of me just couldn't connect those tortured, broken flame infused eyes with someone who would murder his father.

I just couldn't.

A guard stepped in just then, the one that was with me the time I'd served in the fae's section of the prison, and I couldn't stop my heart from leaping with anticipation. Did that mean I was going back there?

I knew I shouldn't feel this way, but I was a little hopeful that seeing him again would cure this ridiculous obsession I'd started to develop.

"Get that cart and get going," the cook who'd been gossiping with me ordered primly, going back to work.

I much too eagerly went to my cart and began to push it behind the guard.

Sure enough, he led me the same way we had gone the other night.

I was going to see him.

The section of the prison was just as depressing as I remembered, and I hurried while I delivered the trays, slipping a few times on the moss covered floor as I tried to get to the fae as quickly as I could. The fact that I couldn't hear any whips or cries this time should have been comforting, but the absolute stillness was a little unsettling. The prisoners that I passed didn't even look up as I delivered the food.

I was a few cells away from what I thought was the fae's, when an angry cry catapulted towards me.

The guard, who had appeared bored this whole time, snapped to attention. "Stay here," he ordered as he set off in the direction of the cry. There were more sounds now, the sounds of destruction. And despite the guard's orders, I followed behind him, leaving the cart behind me.

By the time I'd made it to where the sounds were coming from, the guard had thrown open the cell door and was trying to grab the unruly prisoner.

The unruly prisoner who happened to be the fae.

"Where is it?" he screamed over and over again, clawing at the guard, at himself, at the rocks on the walls.

Chunks of the wall were littered on the floor. The fae was so manic in his movements that the guard couldn't control him. I watched as he radioed for backup.

Still, the fae continued to ask where something was.

What could he have been looking for?

Suddenly he caught sight of me, and there was recognition in his eyes this time.

"You. You need to help me find it. I have to find it," he growled at me nonsensically, his voice almost musical in its foreign inflection.

"What is it? What are you missing?" I found myself

asking through the bars of the cell...much to the guard's displeasure, who had just noticed my presence.

"Get back to your cart," he screeched at me, just as another guard rushed in to help him subdue the wayward fae.

"The crystal. Where is the crystal?" the fae yelled at me as I slowly backed away from the cell. Then the guards began to beat him with batons laced with purple electricity.

"Calm down and get back into your cell."

The fae's hoarse cries surrounded me, and I covered my eyes as great sobs wracked my body at the sound of his pain once again.

Suddenly I froze. A crystal.

I knew where a crystal was. Surely it wasn't the one that the mouse had given me? The one that I'd given the Warden in exchange for a different fate?

It couldn't be.

A sick dread passed over me at the thought that I could have added more pain to this poor creature.

I was only faintly aware of the guard returning and dragging me back to my cart, out of that section of the prison without finishing the rest of my deliveries, and back to my cell.

The odds of me getting that crystal back were about as slim as me getting my power back.

What was I going to do?

* * *

 felt listless for the next few days. I wasn't let out of my cell during that time, I suppose as punishment for disobeying the guard during my food deliveries although no one bothered to tell me that.

I had lost track of how many days I'd been here. You couldn't even depend on when they turned on the lights as being daytime, since the prison liked to fuck with its prisoners by turning them on all hours of the day.

My only friend was the little mouse who visited me, bringing me trinkets I assumed it had stolen from other prisoners. Well, I guess I counted the spider in the corner as my friend as well. We both were wasting our lives doing nothing of importance.

I dozed off for the umpteenth time when all of a sudden, the clang of my prison cell signaled that someone was opening the door. I lazily opened my eyes, not really caring who it was at this point. A guard with green tinged skin I hadn't seen before was standing there, looking affronted that I hadn't jumped to my feet to greet him.

"Come on," he hissed at me, a forked tongue peeking out from his lips as he spoke.

That got me moving. I hadn't seen someone like him before. It was amazing how sheltered I'd been for a would-be prostitute. There were so many creatures in this prison that I'd never come across before. Maybe Julian and his coven were picky about who they sold our services to, because I'd only seen run of the mill creatures, like werewolves and such.

This guard resembled some kind of demon frog, and I couldn't even begin to guess what he was.

I followed after him reluctantly, my muscles weak from doing nothing for so many days. It was amazing how I actually missed delivering food, since it gave me something to do. We weaved through a few hallways, passing by a door that I recognized as belonging to Dr. Brina. I shivered at the sight of the entrance, remembering how strange she'd acted. Then there was the crazy dream I'd experienced afterwards that I wasn't so sure had been just a dream. I breathed a sigh of relief when he made no move to stop at her door.

We did pause at an entrance just down the hall though. The sign on the door said *Prison Psychiatrist*, and I grimaced. Apparently, it was time for my forced shrink session. I could only imagine what kind of psychiatrist I was about to meet in a place like this.

The guard knocked on the door and a high-pitched voice called for us to wait a minute.

I leaned against the wall, examining the guard out of the corner of my eye, still curious what kind of creature he was.

Finally, the door opened and a grim beast of a man in an orange jumpsuit stepped into the hallway. I could tell right away he was some kind of shifter. He seemed agitated, and his eyes kept flicking back and forth from humanesque to beast-like. Evidently, his session hadn't gone well.

"Get in there," my green guard ordered me. I guess he was dropping me off and taking the shifter back to his cell. I gave the shifter a wide berth as I walked to the office entrance. He looked like he was on the edge of shifting any minute, and I didn't want to be around for that.

The room appeared empty at first when I entered. It looked like I envisioned a shrink office to look, based on books I'd read. There was a long, worn looking leather couch in the middle of the room, and the walls were lined with shelves filled to the brim with different colored books. Potted plants were set around the room, and there was a Tiffany lamp sitting on a coffee table by the couch.

"Please sit down," a quiet voice said politely, and I squeaked when I realized there was someone sitting in the room in a leather lounge chair across from the couch. The woman was so tiny and unassuming that she hadn't caught my eye upon entering the room. Her hair was cut in a dark brown bob, and she had perfect porcelain skin that accentuated her red lined lips. Even sitting down, I could tell that she was much smaller than I was. She was dressed professionally, wearing a white blouse tucked in a plaid, fitted pencil skirt with black high heels. Her hands were clasped in her lap, and she was looking down at the floor instead of at me.

I walked to the couch hesitantly. She was not what I expected.

I tried to see if I could sense what she was, but there was a strange blankness emanating from her where there should have been energy. She was once again something that I'd never encountered before. Not even human beings emanated nothing. Then again, I doubt many humans would be comfortable in a place like this.

I shivered. Deciding I probably didn't want to know what she was.

"Thank you for coming here today, Selena," she said softly, still studying the ground.

It was a silly thing to say, since I hadn't had a choice in the matter.

"I'm the prison psychiatrist," she continued. "Dr. Maynard." There was a long pause, as if she didn't know what to say next. "Do you mind if I smoke?" she suddenly asked.

I wasn't partial to cigarette smoke in my face, but I wasn't going to make a fuss in prison, in a room with a creature that was deliberately masking what she was.

"Of course," I responded quietly.

She appeared relieved, opening a small metal box on the table next to her and taking out one of the long cigarettes like the ones that movie stars used to use in the olden days. She struck a match that was also in the box and lit the end of the cigarette, sighing quietly as she took a drag from it.

"I've looked at your file. It appears you were quite the troublemaker before coming here," she commented.

I looked at her in surprise, wondering what was actually written in the file. I guess "wouldn't sleep with Julian" wouldn't have been something they could have put in my file.

"Is there anything in particular you want to talk about? Any problems you've been having?" she asked.

"You mean besides the fact that I'm trapped in Nightmare Penitentiary in the first place?" I responded dryly.

A wisp of a smile appeared briefly on her lovely face. "Yes, besides that, Selena."

I didn't intend on saying anything. I didn't trust anyone who worked here. Especially a creature that was intentionally not showing her real self. That alone left me uneasy.

"Not much to say," I finally answered when the silence stretched on for too long.

"Hmm," she murmured, picking up a file that I assumed was mine. She flicked through the pages. "It appears you've been on lockdown after an incident with one of the prisoners. Do you want to talk about that?" she asked, finally looking up at me.

She must have been talking about what happened with the fae...although I guess I could have had a delayed punishment based on what happened with Alaric as well. But it was probably the fae.

My lips pursed as I remembered for the thousandth time the pain in his voice as he screamed for his crystal...the crystal that I'd traded away.

"You seem like you have something on your mind?" she said, watching me.

"I was just thinking that regret is a funny thing," I answered.

"What do you mean?"

"I mean you can regret something, even if it was an accident. That seems to happen quite often," I responded.

"Hmm. I suppose that's right." she paused. "'There was a long hard time when I kept far from me the remembrance of what I had thrown away when I was quite ignorant of its worth,'" she quoted.

"What's that from?" I asked, confused.

"Charles Dickens. I find human literature so fascinating."

"I thought you were reading my mind for a second," I told her, thinking of how I had no idea the worth of the crystal when I traded it...I still had no idea what exactly it's purpose was.

"I know you don't want to be here, but I'll leave you with a few words of advice before you go," she told me. "It doesn't do well to let yourself be defined by your regrets. We always have a choice."

She stood up just then, as if she hadn't said anything of importance, and strode to the door to let me out. "I think it would be good for us to meet again, Selena," she told me, opening the door where I saw the green guard and another, different prisoner, waiting outside.

She didn't seem like she expected an answer, and I didn't think I had a choice whether I visited her or not, so I walked out without saying anything further.

Her words pounded in my head as the guard led me back to my cell.

She may be a psychiatrist, but she gave shit advice.

Because in truth, I never had a choice.

CHAPTER 12

*D*ays passed.

And more days.

Then, my solitary confinement finally ended.

I fell into a routine, a routine that cemented the fact that I was trapped in this prison for the next year. A year that felt like forever.

Sleep.

Food delivery.

Avoiding inmates, especially the men who'd caught my eye more than they should.

Sleep again. This was my only escape from reality.

Getting up in the morning was becoming a chore. Reminding myself I had a purpose despite being stuck in this hellhole of a place grew harder with each passing day. The dark walls were becoming unbearable, it felt as though they were closing in around me. Choking me. Wearing me down.

I'd even gone back to the library only to find the doors locked—no matter what time of the day I visited —which only added to my mood. I was drowning in here, suffocating. There was no fresh air, no windows to look outside, and refocusing on my job as a food deliverer just wasn't cutting it. I'd only been here a few weeks, and already, I felt like a caged wolf ready to burst free.

Lying on my cot, I stared up at the gray ceiling of my cell, having returned here after breakfast delivery, unsure what I wanted to do to fill my day. Something to tame that growing void inside of me that threatened to send me spiraling into madness.

A squeak came from behind me, and I rolled onto my stomach to look up. My little friend, the light brown mouse with a white face stared at me from where he perched on the metal frame of my cot. At the top of my pillow sat someone's white toothbrush, the bristles worn and bent outward from overuse.

"Who did you steal that from today?"

A faint squeak responded. If there was one thing I had been enjoying, it was my regular visits from this little guy.

"One day, you'll get caught, my friend," I murmured, no longer feeling silly about talking to a mouse.

He turned and scurried across the frame and hopped down before vanishing somewhere under my bed.

The tiny kleptomaniac mouse found a way to keep

himself occupied while trapped in here, even if it involved taking other people's belongings, which was exactly what I had to do. I needed a distraction, not the stealing part... but something that kept my mind occupied.

Up on my feet, I collected the toothbrush and walked it over to the two metal shelves bolted to the opposite wall. I lifted my pile of folded uniforms in reds and orange fabrics, and I pulled out a small cardboard box tucked underneath. Inside lay all the gifts the mouse had brought me. Feathers, a ring, a clump of fur, a scrunched up piece of paper with the words, *"there is no escape"* on it, a sock, and somehow he'd even dragged a studded leather collar in here. They all sat in the box, and I added the toothbrush inside.

The mouse's first gift came to mind... the teal crystal. Along with me giving it to the Warden, and then discovering it belonged to my tortured fae.

I gave away the one thing he seemed to cherish above all else.

I once again remembered his panic stricken expression as he ripped apart his cell to find the missing crystal. I couldn't bring myself to say anything at that moment.

Guilt hit me, and I tightened my grip on the box's lid. This was why I now held onto everything the mouse brought me. No matter what it was, the items belonged to someone, and I'd find a way to return them to the rightful owners. Including finding a way to get that crystal back for the fae... somehow. I hadn't worked that part out yet, as I doubted getting into the Warden's office was an easy feat...or even possible.

But maybe figuring that puzzle out was the distraction I needed. Closing the box, I tucked it back under my clothes and headed over to the sink to wash myself with a damp cloth. I left my orange prison pajamas on as I washed, since my door was open like everyone else's. Not many inmates wandered past my room, but it still left me uncomfortable to be so exposed.

I finished washing and dressed in fresh orange prison pants and a black tank top over my bra. I then stepped into my grungy tennis shoes that were the standard issue in my section of the prison.

"Perfect timing," Keon's deep voice came from behind me.

I could hear the smile in his tone before I even turned around, and immediately, my body reacted. Burning fire licked the length of my spine, my nipples stiffening and rubbing against the fabric of my bra.

I turned, wondering how long he'd been standing there. I hadn't seen him during my punishment, but I'd sometimes sensed eyes watching me at night from the darkness. I'd always hoped that it was him, rather than some other creep I didn't know. The creep you knew was always better than the one you didn't.

Keon had a shoulder pressed into the doorframe, hands deep into his uniform pants, navy blue today, and one leg crossed over the other at the ankle. His dark chestnut hair was brushed off his face with a few loose strands draped over an eye. A shadow of stubble graced his jawline. And those piercing green eyes were a contrast to his tanned skin, while the corners of his lips quirked upward.

"Perfect for what?" I asked, unable to look away from the angles on his face, the muscles. This man was all brawn and desire and utterly gorgeous. I clenched my thighs together to stem off the arousal. He shouldn't be affecting me this way, and I shouldn't be remembering what his lips tasted like. Then again, I fell victim to Alaric too—though to be fair, he was an incubus. While I thought I lured these men to me, he in fact, tricked me and fed off me. Sexy asshole.

With Keon, it was different. I'd given myself to him freely. And now… well, now I struggled to make sense of my emotions around him.

My mother always warned me against falling for men...although really, it was a bit hypocritical, since I was pretty sure she'd been in love with Julian for a long time. *They are attracted to your lure as a siren. Not who you are.*

Her words always stayed with me and were probably why I never allowed myself to get too close to any guys. Well that, and the fact that Julian never really gave me the chance.

Keon and I studied each other. With the way he looked at me, he didn't have to say anything, everything was there in his eyes. Hunger. Eagerness. Confidence that I was his.

He knew what he wanted, and he stared at me like he was going hunting and I was his intended prey.

"I have something to show you," he said casually, glancing at me as curiosity bloomed on my face.

I snorted a laugh as I ran my fingers through my hair, swooping the long, dark strands over my shoulder to try and work through the knots. Not having a comb was certainly inconvenient. "You know that sounded a bit creepy."

He shrugged. "All depends on how you interpret the words."

"So, are you off duty right now?" I asked, and stepped closer to him, my body heating up from his presence alone.

"When I'm in here, I'm always on duty, little shadow." He straightened and stepped out of my cell. "You coming?"

A slither of panic slid down my skin. It was an unreasonable fear on my part. He'd saved me...still, uncertainty sat heavy on my chest. At the same time, I didn't want him to leave me alone. As he stepped farther away, my stomach knotted.

I should have said no, excused myself, anything but step outside my cell to follow him. I gave into my own curiosity to find out what he wanted to show me. Gave in to my fear of being left alone with my dark thoughts.

Mother Goddess, he was handsome. It seemed to be

the only thought consuming me. For those moments when he came to my cell, I had forgotten about the heaviness in my chest, about the darkness fraying the edges of my mind. Keon offered me a chance to forget it all, and I took the opportunity.

CHAPTER 13

Once we left the main area of cells behind, his hand slipped into mine, and he quickly guided me down a corridor, sticking to the shadows. We moved fast, taking corridors left and right, and I made a mental note of the turns, tucking them into my mind.

When he finally stopped, he glanced over his shoulder at me and smiled. His smile was a bit devilish, like we were about to do something we shouldn't. The jangle of keys drew my attention to his hand as he jammed an old-fashioned long key into the hole and unlocked the door. He quickly drew me inside by my hand before locking us inside.

"I'm surprised this place still uses keys," I said, glancing around the dimly lit room and remembering the blood sacrifice that one of the walls in the prison had required.

There was a double bed, freshly made. A table with four chairs and a deck of playing cards in the middle along with a bowl of candy. A bar fridge in the corner.

Without asking, I hurried over and took a handful of the small round candies and popped them into my mouth. They melted on my tongue, and I moaned from the sweet taste. I had missed out on candy growing up. My mother would be horrified if she saw me now, but I didn't care. I was in a freaking prison, so I'd eat whatever the hell I wanted.

"Got a sweet tooth?" Keon asked.

I collected another handful and turned to face him. "I assume this candy is free for the taking?"

He nodded, smiling divinely. I adored the way he looked at me like nothing else in the world existed. We hardly knew each other, yet in his company, I felt content. Maybe I was completely fucked up on the inside. Broken. Lost. Or I was so desperate for affection, I clung to whatever little bit was offered to me.

Except, what he was feeling probably wasn't real. I wasn't a fool to think he was different from all the others who were pulled in by my abilities. I wanted to believe Keon liked me for me, but it really wasn't probable. I wasn't even sure it was possible.

As much as I tried to deny it, prison life had been unexpected. I'd been terrified to come to this prison, expecting only fear and panic. Yet somehow, I'd found myself attracted to the monsters in here... guards and criminals alike. Dangerous men. Seductive men.

Keon wasn't the only one who drove me crazy with need.

Maybe there was something wrong with me, or maybe I had to admit to myself that I was captivated by the darker side these men offered me.

"What is this room?" I popped the rest of the candy into my mouth, savoring the fruity sweetness once more. I was probably going to eat the whole bowl.

"My secret haven. A place a few of us guards hang out without cameras watching. I'd be happy to bring you here when you need some time away."

"Oh." My gaze drifted to the door and back. "So anyone can pop in here and find me?"

"Don't worry. No one's coming. We're alone," he said, standing tall. "Only I have the keys today."

No barriers stood between us, and if he wanted to, he could slit my throat. I regretted having that thought immediately because he'd only ever saved me. He wasn't the predator here, but my savior. He was the only person I felt comfortable coming to, despite the situation of how we first met. That was only solidified when he saved me from the vampire.

I glanced up at him, meeting those hypnotizing green eyes. "I'm not scared, if that's what you think." I held myself taller.

He strolled closer, and I didn't react until he stood inches from me and his hand cupped the side of my face. He combed his hand through my hair and fisted my hair at the back of my head. Then he tilted my chin up. I should have cried out, but instead, I found myself falling into those green, green pools in his eyes. They promised me escape, a place to abandon myself and forget the horrible place I ended up in.

"Maybe you should be scared," he murmured.

A bolt of electricity filled me at his touch. I stared up at him, holding his gaze. My knees trembled beneath me.

"I can smell your fear. I see it in the way your eyes flick about nervously. I can hear it in the faint strain of your voice." His tone was mocking and rough, and I couldn't help the way my body responded to the sound of it, heat spiraling through me. I shouldn't be turned on by this show of aggression, but I was. My breath caught in my lungs.

"So, I can come here any time to hang out, you say?" I mouthed nervously, not sure I trusted myself right now from dragging him closer and kissing him. Except, that was exactly what my body wanted. What I craved.

"Of course," he answered, overzealous in his quick response. "I haven't been able to get you out of my head since that night. I want you, Selena. I'll do anything to have you," he continued, a hint of desperation in his voice.

I want you. Those three words resonated within my mind. I've had boys say them to me in the past at school, many in fact. They'd all been blinded by the call of my siren. And maybe Keon was blinded too right now… I didn't know. But I didn't want to know at that moment. I needed his closeness and to extinguish the flames roaring through my body. I wanted to pretend this was real for just a little while.

The thought of walking away and doing the right thing crossed my mind, but with it came a disturbing ache in my stomach. An unease settled through me at leaving Keon.

I wished I didn't feel so weak, so vulnerable, so eager for him.

Instead of pulling away, I watched the twitch of his lips as he leaned closer. I could have turned away. I should have. But I did nothing.

Our mouths crushed together. His lips demanding, his tongue forcing past the seam of my lips. Desire flooded me, eroding my resistance.

He broke from me, smirking, his eyes seeming to have changed to a lighter shade of green.

"Your taste…" He licked his lower lip, his eyes rolling up momentarily like he floated on his own cloud of euphoria. "I've never tasted a siren before."

I blinked at his words. He knew what I was. Of course he'd find out from my prison records, and it made me smile to know he liked me enough that he'd checked up on me. It would be exactly what I would do too.

"You know what I am, but what are you?"

Instead of answering, he kissed me again. I trembled. My lips tingled, and I couldn't stop thinking about how he tasted, how I thought I might explode from the heat coursing through me.

It was exhilarating.

Heart stopping.

Arousing.

Fireworks went off through my body.

My mind whirled, heart raced. Everything about him won me over.

He stood over me, his large body blocking everything. When he broke from my lips, he stared down at me with a primal, savage look.

"You are mine, Selena," he murmured as his hands settled on my waist. He lifted me off my feet and claimed my mouth.

I wrapped my arms around his neck, clinging to him, drowning beneath his desire. I inhaled his masculine scent. There was something inside of him, something dark that curled around me. It teased me with a sliver of fear… something unknown.

"I want to be yours," I whispered against his mouth. I'd been so down lately, and he offered me an escape from the hell I lived in.

The delicious growling sound he made told me he liked my response. He licked my lips, tasting me hungrily.

"Yes, you will be," he moaned as he laid me on the bed. "And I'll be everything you need."

He didn't waste a moment and kneeled on the

mattress. He leaned over me and captured my mouth with his.

I cupped the sides of his face, completely lost to this beautifully sexy man. A memory of how Alaric had felt flashed through my mind, but I pushed it away, focusing all my concentration on Keon.

Breathing was close to impossible, as was thinking straight. I didn't care about anything but being with him. The man who took my virginity. There would always be a special place for him in my heart, and I'd never forget him.

He kissed me all over my face, his body pressed to mine. I pulled at the buttons on his jacket, popping them open. I wanted to feel his skin against mine. To feel what really lay underneath his clothes.

His large hands pulled my top up to my chest and tucked under me to my back. I arched myself as he unclipped my bra.

I sucked in rapid breaths and squeezed my thighs together as excitement blew through me.

He lowered himself, and his mouth found the soft skin of my stomach, covering it in kisses before cutting a path to my breasts. Quickly, he dragged my bra and top up over my body and head.

With my hands above me, the fabric of my top still covering my face, he settled a hand over my arms and stilled me. "Don't move gorgeous, stay right there."

His words stole my breath, leaving me shuddering.

Cool air licked over my skin. I drowned under his attention.

His large hands found my breasts and kneaded them. His mouth pressed to mine, the fabric of my shirt between our kiss. Black material was all I could see. Heat engulfed me as he held me down. All the while, his hand swept down my body and slipped under the elastic of my pants and underwear.

My breath hitched as shivers encased me. His fingers found the slickness of my heat, and he rubbed me until my legs widened for him. I arched at his touch, my hips rocking back and forth.

I was trapped by him, by his touch. His tongue traveled down the valley of my breasts before he found the pointed peak of my nipples.

I gasped, the fabric of my top sticking to my face from the warmth of my rushed breaths.

"I want you naked and under me, begging me for more." His voice was dark and violent.

My heart pounded in my ears like a thousand drums.

"You deserve so much more," he murmured, pulling his hand away from my core. The bed shifted beneath me to indicate he stood up. He lifted one of my feet and pulled a shoe off, then he did the same with the other foot. Next thing, his fingers curled under the top of my pants, and he dragged them down my legs, along with my underwear.

An inferno engulfed me as I lay spread out before him, my face still covered.

Footsteps brought him up beside me as he gently tugged away the top and bra trapping me. He tossed them to the floor.

I breathed in and looked up at him, still completely dressed while I lay there vulnerable. His pupils had completely dilated, and there was something almost feral behind his gaze. Was he a shifter?

"You're so fucking beautiful, Selena." He shouldered his jacket off and let it drop to the ground behind him. Underneath he wore a tight tee that pulled taut across a broad, powerful chest. "I have so much to make up for after our first time together in the bar."

"It was perfect for me."

He studied me as he reached down and collected my hand and placed it to his mouth. He kissed my palm, then stretched my arm up to the metal bedhead. There he pulled out a leather handcuff already attached to the bed. He wrapped the band around my wrist before tying it up where it wasn't so tight that it hurt.

"Is this okay?" He walked around the bed to my other hand.

My brain wasn't working. Not while my body pulsed with arousal. "Yes," I breathed, drawing my knees up, squeezing my thighs together.

"Good." He tied my other arm to the top of the bed.

He stood back and stared down at my naked body. A dirty smirk played across his lips, and I buzzed all over, adoring the way he stared at me like he was trying to get himself under control. A groan spilled from his mouth, the corded muscles in his neck clenched.

Something about Keon made me feel alive, dissolving the depressing thoughts constantly plaguing my mind. I was tired of feeling numb, spiraling into darkness. I wanted him to make me feel.

"I need you," I murmured. "Please, Keon."

His hand slipped to the side of my face. "My little shadow, I'll give you everything I have and more." Complicated emotions flickered in his gaze, something deep and heartfelt.

The sharp edge of my desire seized my thoughts.

All that filled me was a savage lust.

And I forgot everything else.

I saw the same need in his gaze. We were more alike than I first thought. In a few long strides, he moved to the end of the bed then climbed on. Hands on my knees, he jerked them open, his gaze plunging to my heat.

There was a twitch at the corners of his mouth as he dropped down on all fours before my spread legs. He kissed the insides of my thighs, taking mock bites, making his way lower.

I threw my head back onto the bed, crying out with anticipation.

His mouth covered the perfect spot, ripping a moan from my mouth. He lapped at me, drawing even more heat from me. I needed him there. My pelvis rocked up and down, pushing myself against his face. Against that sexy tongue that devoured me.

"Oh, fuck, yes!"

With a brutal jerk of my hips, he lifted them as he rose to his knees. My legs hung up and over the back of his shoulders. His mouth latched to my pussy while those devious eyes looked at me as he ate me. So focused and intense, he watched me writhe and groan.

In a heartbeat, he pulled back. His mouth and chin glistened, and he clicked his lips hungrily.

"Fuck, Selena. Your pussy is gorgeous."

I could barely catch my breath as he gently lowered my ass and legs back to the bed. My heart raced, and every inch of me purred.

"Please, fuck me," I begged, feeling desperate for him to push me over the ledge I was standing at the edge of.

Keon climbed off the bed, his pants tenting from his huge erection. "I love your dirty mouth." He stalked across the room before he pulled open a drawer near the bed. In his hand, he held a long black box, then flipped open the lid.

I craned my neck up, my hands straining against the cuff so I could easily see what was inside. He turned away from me and headed to the side of the bed before taking a seat. My eyes caught the black dildo in his hand.

My eyes grew wide incredulously.

"Want to play?"

"I..." The rest of my words fell away.

"First time?" He chuckled and kneeled on the bed at my feet. "Open up for me gorgeous."

My legs fell open, the need for him still humming through me. The way he'd devoured me left me tingling and ready to burst. His fingers ran the length of my slickness before he inserted two inside me.

I arched, groaning with desire, my hips raising to meet his touch. My mind already floated on euphoria.

"You're ready," he told me, before quickly replacing his fingers with the dildo. It was slick and glided into me, filling me.

A rasping groan fell from his lips. When I looked at him, he had so much devious desire in his eyes as he focused on filling me completely. There was so much lust in his eyes, so much excitement, so much everything. With a flick, the dildo began to vibrate.

"Oh crap," I purred loudly. My skin tightened. The sensation was impossible to describe, but it felt like my insides trembled. I writhed on the bed, my thighs drawing closed.

"No, no, I want to see you open."

Then he got off the bed and stared at his handiwork before pulling out a phone from his back pocket.

Panic hit me straight in the chest.

I jerked against the restraints. "What are you doing?"

"It's okay angel. I just need a close-up image

because I never want to forget. I want to have your pussy being fucked by a vibrator to view."

Before I could respond, he leaned in close and snapped a shot of my quivering body.

"That better not be sent to anyone else."

"Fuck, that is going to set me off every time I look at it." He pulled himself back up. "For my eyes only. That sweet cunt is all mine."

He jerked the fabric of his tee up and over his body, revealing the most exquisite muscular torso. Lines of sharp angles, ribbed stomach, and not a sign of hair.

I drowned in lust, feeling like I was in some kind of fantasy as I watched him strip in front of me as his toy continued to torture me.

He unlatched the utility belt around his waist and popped open the button of his pants. In no time, he dropped them and kicked them aside along with his boots.

My attention drifted to his thick, hard shaft that stood upright and erect. He gripped his cock and drew the skin back and forth two times, his eyes rolling back with lust.

"You ready for me?"

"Please," I begged.

He moved over the top of me and with a flick of his hand, he withdrew the vibrator. A pulse flared to life deep in my gut. I glanced up at him as he stared at me intently. The tip of his dick pressed to my entrance.

Adrenaline laced my pulse. He leaned forward and claimed me as he drove into me.

I moaned against his mouth, tasting myself on his tongue. Sweet and musky with a slight edge. My legs widened for him, my hips tilting upward for easy access.

He thrusted into me with incredible stamina and strength. My core pulsed under him, my lips swollen. I shuddered as he fucked me with primal need.

The way he drove into me was savage, and yet, he kissed me tenderly. I cried out from the intensity of his friction, the sheer size of him stretching me with each plunge.

I wanted my hands free so that I could run them all over his body. Instead, I drew his lower lip into my mouth and bit it. I tasted the metallic sharpness of his blood, but he never once complained or stopped moving. Goosebumps erupted over my skin.

He growled with arousal, the strong cords of his neck clenching.

Pleasure surged through me faster and faster. It built, flaring to life. Sparks of white light crashed over my mind, dragging me under.

I caught Keon's expression, how lost he was in the moment too. He was so sexy, so manly, so fucking delicious.

Both of us heaved for breath, covered in sweat as we moved against each other. The room smelled of seductive sex.

In a perfect moment of utter bliss, a climax caught me by complete surprise. It crashed through me like a storm. Ripping me apart.

Liquid fire rushed through me, and my core clenched around Keon's cock.

I screamed, my head thrown back, my whole body tightening as I floated on the after effect of my climax.

"Fuck, Selena," he roared, a muscle ticking in his jaw. "That's right, suck my cock with that tight pussy." His groan filled the room as he pulsed inside me.

Our breaths raced, and we clung to one another. I couldn't stop smiling. "You're incredible."

"Fuck me, you're a vision," he growled as he stared at me with an expression of complete admiration. He swooped in closer and covered my face in kisses. "You've done something to me," he admitted. "And I don't think I can ever let you walk away now."

If I wasn't collapsed on the bed, tied up and breathing heavily from a mind-blowing orgasm, I might have found his words overly possessive. Except, I came here to escape and forget everything else. Keon gave me what I craved and needed. Just as he had back at the bar.

Once again, I wanted to believe his feelings were real...but how could I ever really know?

His breath grazed my ear. "You ready to go again, my little shadow? Would you like that?"

I met the savagery of his gaze, the eagerness to take me over and over. I wanted to keep inhaling his scent, to never stop feeling the sensation of his skin sliding over mine. I couldn't get enough of that roughness when he fucked me.

"Yes," I eagerly answered.

* * *

I woke up in bed in my prison cell. Last thing I remembered was falling asleep on Keon's chest in his secret room after the kinkiest sex ever. It never occurred to me being tied up would drive me so crazy, but it was insanely amazing.

Keon must have carried me back to my room afterward.

I glanced across my dimly lit room to see the door was closed, meaning it was night. Panic flashed through my mind. I missed my delivery shift. Hell! I prayed Keon gave them a reason for me not turning up. I'd be at the kitchens first thing in the morning for my next shift. I didn't want any excuse for them to insist I wasn't working out or for the Warden to go back on his word about me working in the kitchen.

From across the room on the floor, a fashion magazine I'd picked up from Alessia caught my attention. One of the featured stories was titled, 'love made people stronger.'

I never grew up in a normal home, and I wasn't even sure if my mother ever really loved me. Maybe she did... in her own way. But the world I grew up in was filled with hate and fear, and admitting love was being defiant.

What I felt for Keon couldn't be love… but whatever it was, he had my heart racing, my stomach exploding with butterflies at the thought of him. It was just a crush…right?

I pulled the blanket off when a sting flared across my ankle.

"Ouch." I bent my leg and drew my foot in closer.

"What the hell?" There was a black, five pointed star inked on the inside of my ankle about the size of my fingernail. The rest of the skin around it blushed. I looked closer, my mouth dropping open. That definitely wasn't there before.

I ran a thumb over the mark, finding my skin still sensitive and slightly raised.

"Fuck!" Keon tattooed me? Was he fucking kidding?

I shoved myself out of bed and marched to the sink. Lifting my foot, I placed it awkwardly into the sink and ran water over my ankle. With soap, I rubbed the hell out of the star. I gritted my teeth through the pain, furious that Keon would do this like I was his property or something. Who else would sneak into my room to brand me? And how did I not feel it happening?

The cold water washed over my ankle. But all I achieved was making my skin redder with irritation. The star remained, and I sighed heavily.

Drying off, I headed back to bed and slumped into

it, crossing my legs in front of me. I looked down at the mark incredulously.

I couldn't even begin to make sense why he'd do this, or the fury burning through my veins. When I saw him next, I was going to kill him.

CHAPTER 14

That same grumpy guard was waiting for me outside of the kitchens, and my heart tripped over itself. I was going to see my fae again.

"Don't do anything stupid this time," he warned me as we walked through the entrance of the "crypt" as I'd started referring to this section of the prison. It reminded me a little of pictures of the catacombs in France that I'd seen once. I couldn't stop the shivers that curled down my spine as I took a step inside.

I did my job, delivering the plates of decaying slop to the prisoners. We'd only made it past a few cells, when the guard suddenly peered through the bars of the cell I'd just passed food into. The prisoner was laying on his stomach, wearing nothing but rags, almost unrecognizable as a living creature, since he was so covered in filth.

But was he living? Fear flickered in my stomach as I noticed the unsettling way he wasn't moving at all.

"Fuck," the guard muttered, unlocking the cell and rushing inside. He held a hand to the man's neck, assumedly checking for a pulse. He cursed again, and my stomach dropped even more.

The guard yelled into his earpiece for medical and then started shaking the prisoner, as if that was going to bring him to life. Just two minutes later, a medical team hustled past me into the cell and started to work on him. I didn't think anything was going to work.

Realizing that no one was paying attention to me, I couldn't resist the urge to walk the few cells over and see the fae. There were no sounds coming from his cell, and I was relieved to see him sitting against the wall, idly scratching the floor with a small piece of rock. He didn't look up until I'd been standing there for at least a minute. But when he saw me, recognition flared through him.

"You," he said calmly. I just gulped, momentarily tongue tied at the fact that he'd spoken to me.

"Hi," I finally replied lamely.

"You watch me," he stated, staring at me avidly. And I couldn't do anything but nod. I was caught in the trance of those flickering blue fire eyes of his.

"I can't help it," I answered, wanting to crawl into a hole after I admitted that sorry fact.

Something flashed through his eyes. Surprise maybe?

"What's your name?" he asked.

"Selena."

He repeated my name, almost seeming to savor the word as he said it.

"I think I took something from you," I blurted out.

Faster than I could blink, he was suddenly standing in front of me, only the bars keeping him from me.

"What did you take?" he asked.

"I was given a crystal on my first night here," I stammered, overcome with the fury flooding his beautiful face.

He reached through the bars and a blue electricity started to race through his skin from the bars. He just gritted his teeth though and continued to reach for me.

"Give it to me," he ordered imperiously, desperation leaking out of his countenance though, despite his tone.

"It's gone," I gasped out.

He watched me for a minute more, his teeth clenching at the electricity that was still pulsing through him.

All of a sudden, he pulled away, his shoulders drooping as he turned away from me and walked back to sit against the wall. He didn't look at me again.

Someone grabbed my arm just then, and I whirled around to see that it was the irate looking guard.

"You need to get back to your cell while I finish dealing with this. The cameras will be watching you, and if I find out you tried anything else, I'll make sure you're left in your cell for a month this time around," the guard threatened, and I nodded and hurried away, noting briefly that the medical team was still working furiously on the prisoner.

I should have gone to my cell. A week in solitary confinement had felt like a year, but I pressed on, walking my cart determinedly until I found a guard. "I'm supposed to deliver these to the maximum security section," I said while motioning to my still full cart.

The maximum security section was not going to like their food today.

The guard looked confused for a moment, but I'd seen him before, and he knew that I delivered food to various places in the prison.

"Where's Gastod?" he asked, and I just shrugged my shoulders, assuming it was the grumpy guard he was talking about.

"Fine, I'll take you," he snapped, beginning to walk away and expecting that I would follow him. I did dutifully, even across the swinging bridge and through the blood hungry wall.

I moved quickly, not looking any of the prisoners in the eye, since I was delivering rotting food to them instead of the meatloaf they were supposed to be eating today. I was especially embarrassed when I served Sinclair her meal. She knew it was meatloaf day.

Finally, I arrived at Alaric's cell. I ignored the lust that shot through me at just the sight of him.

He gave me a lazy smile. "I've been wondering when I'd see you again," he drawled.

"I need a favor from you," I whispered, skipping niceties as I glanced at the guard who was a few feet away from me, fiddling with something on his phone.

"Favors cost things," he said, eyeing me up and down. "What do I get in return?"

"What do you want?" I carefully answered, somehow knowing that you didn't enter into deals with this incubus lightly.

"I'll let you know," he said. "But first, I want to hear what you want."

I felt desperate for some reason. I had no idea why I was so desperate to help the fae, but I was.

"I need you to steal something from the Warden's office," I said quietly, shooting another glance at the guard who was still occupied and hadn't even noticed how long I'd been at this one cell.

Alaric started laughing uproariously, startling the guard and all this row's occupants with how loud and boisterous he was. He'd walked up to the bars to talk to me, but now he turned away, still laughing as he settled himself back on his cot.

"You can ask your boy toy for that one, baby," he said, crossing his legs in front of him and tucking his arms behind his head as he continued to chuckle.

"Please," I begged. "I'll do anything."

He seemed to think on that for a minute, but then shook his head.

"When I choose to piss off the Warden, it will be because I've escaped, not because I was doing something stupid like stealing from him. Everyone knows that shadow demons don't share," he answered.

I opened my mouth to beg once more, but the guard was there, pushing me forward. I looked back at Alaric desperately, and he just winked at me.

Bastard.

I was thoroughly depressed as we finished passing out trays, and I began to walk back to my cell.

Suddenly, another guard was there, stopping us.

"The Warden wants to see you," the guard barked, and I panicked. Had he somehow heard already what I'd asked Alaric about stealing from his office? What was he going to do to me?

Fear spiked through me as the new guard immediately began to lead me toward the Warden's office.

What the fuck had I done?

CHAPTER 15

I knocked on the enormous black door that seemed to change every time I visited the Warden. Today, the wood was ornately carved with snakes at the corners and a glorious oak tree in the middle. It was beautiful in a macabre kind of way.

A guard stood nearby, watching me intently as if I might change my mind and run away. He leered at me, and I realized I misinterpreted his creepy interest for something else. He wanted me to try to leave, to give him any reason to give chase. The glint in his pale yellow eyes screamed wolf. Thick brows pulled together over narrowing eyes. I wouldn't give him the satisfaction of hunting me down.

"Come in," the Warden finally barked from inside his office.

Hastily, I pushed open the door and left the gawking guard behind me. Before shutting the door behind me, I caught him blowing me a kiss. What the heck?

I turned around and stepped deeper into the office.

Each time I visited this room, I was in awe by the shelves and shelves of collectable ornaments. The idea of spending a whole week in this office wouldn't be enough for me to explore every single object.

My gaze drifted directly to my siren orb on the top shelf near the Warden's desk. The golden waves inside swayed as if sensing my presence, calling to me. Goosebumps peppered my skin in response. There was something disturbing about having a part of myself taken and kept just out of reach. I'd only carried my song ability with me for one day, but in that short time, I felt more complete than I ever had. It was who I was meant to be. Strong, confident, and in control.

Most of my life had been anything but in my control.

My fingers tingled with the need to take back what belonged to me. To embrace my full power.

I looked around at all the objects filling this room, trying to distract myself... all of the items most likely had their own stories to tell. Like the teal crystal from the fae.

I squirmed on the inside with the memory of what I'd done, and after meeting him, it made my guilt a thousand times worse.

"This isn't a museum tour," the Warden snapped, and I swept my gaze toward him as I moved with quick steps to his desk. I took a seat across the desk from him.

He wore a heavy leather coat of deep brown, with bulging pockets, and what looked like plated small armor on his shoulders. If he wasn't wearing a shirt underneath with a black tie, I might have easily guessed he was a drug lord from the seedy streets of Chicago.

The man rubbed a hand over his jawline, which was covered in three-day growth. Today, he appeared disheveled and irritated. A permanent crease sat on the bridge of his nose as he studied me.

"I've heard you're a hard worker." He reclined in his seat, the leather of his jacket groaning. "That you don't complain and do what's needed. That's a good trait to have, Selena."

"I'm keeping my end of the bargain," I answered. "As we agreed." As much as I'd like to follow my gut instinct and steal back what belonged to me, that was nothing more than pure temptation. It would land me in a world of trouble. I was practically on Hell's doorstep already.

He eyed me intently, then a smirk cracked his stoic expression. "Good. I was hoping I wouldn't have to change my mind about our arrangement."

This whole time he doubted me? I could only imagine what lies Julian had told the Warden about me. What horrible mistruths that made me seem worse than I was. Just like my records the psychiatrist mentioned.

Was the Warden waiting for me to fail, for an opportunity, so he could change his mind? Did he call me into his office to remind me that he held my power, and I was simply another pawn under his thumb?

I knew he compromised whatever business relationship he had with Julian by going against his wishes and putting me on food delivery service. So, I hoped he wasn't having second thoughts.

I shifted in my seat uncomfortably.

When the Warden didn't say anything but simply stared at me, I said, "I promise to continue working hard. Is that all?" I shifted to the edge of my seat, ready to run out of here and stop feeling like a bug under a microscope.

"No." He leaned forward, resting his forearms on the table, moving a bit too close to me for my liking.

With only a short distance between us, I could see the golden flecks in his dark eyes that seemed to move around his irises. The brackets around his mouth deepened as he smiled. The look he gave me hit me hard, because I knew what it meant. I'd seen Julian wear this same mask many times.

The Warden wanted something from me.

I pushed back into my seat, knowing I wasn't going anywhere fast, and waited for the news to drop. My stomach churned with anticipation. Did he want me to do something that involved sexual favors for someone? Did *he* want sexual favors from me? I gritted my teeth because I would walk into Hell before I did any of that.

His eyes narrowed. "I need to ask a favor of you."

And there it was. My gut tightened, and I held my breath, waiting for the *favor* that would somehow make my life here even more unbearable.

"You recently visited Seth, the only fae in our penitentiary, and I was told you had a very calming effect on him. Is this right?"

I stiffened, confused at first by what he was saying.

Seth. So that was the fae's name.

Even if the guilt of what I'd done gnawed on me, there was this level of separation between us without knowing his name. I didn't really know him... but now that I had his name, it made it ten times worse.

Seth.

He was no longer just *the fae*. Now it felt personal. A name gave someone an identity and a presence. There was power in a name. We once had a mouse in the mansion back home, and the moment my mother named him, we couldn't kill him. So, he ended up being the family pet.

I groaned under my breath, wishing the Warden hadn't told me the fae's name.

Now when I heard his name, all I'd think about was the extra anguish I caused him. Of course, it was an accident, but that thought didn't eliminate the hurt in my chest. All I could picture was the sorrow on his face, as though the crystal was the only thing he had left in this world.

"I tried to help him," I said. "He was distraught when I last saw him."

The Warden's eyes narrowed as he studied me for a long moment.

I blinked at him and prompted him to tell me what favor he wished from me. "What would you like me to do? Comfort him more?"

With a curt shake of his head, he said, "There's information I need from Seth, but he's not in the right state of mind to tell me."

"Like a secret?" I asked, my voice trembling because the stories I'd heard of the fae and their secrets never ended well. They were always complicated and filled with drama, and revenge. Everything came with revenge for them.

His mouth pinched at the corners. "More like where he's hiding something."

I still couldn't get my head around why he was asking me this. I didn't know Seth. We were both in fact locked in a cage.

As if he picked up on my confusion, he said, "You have a very calming nature, Selena. And with your siren ability to attract, it will be easy for you to get to know Seth, for him to trust you. I'll give you unlimited access to spend time with him. We've amped up our torture tactics lately and I'm sure he'll be grateful for anything...or anyone that gives him a break."

My stomach twisted in knots as I remembered Seth's anger when I told him that I had the crystal. And on top of that, he'd murdered a king. Well, it was rumored he did that, but he was in this prison for a reason, right? And now the Warden wanted me to get close and cozy with him?

"I'm not sure how I feel about deceiving him. Why would he tell me his secrets anyway?"

The Warden exhaled loudly, frustration furrowing his brow. "It's simple, Selena. You get to know him, win over his confidence, and then you will find out where he's put his father's scepter. It was hidden after the murder." He stared at me with that same look he had when he negotiated for the crystal. Ruthless and callous.

"Scepter?" Now I was even more confused. "What's so special about this scepter?"

"The light fae can't appoint a new king without it. So I've agreed to help them. And you will help me," he said firmly.

I doubted I had a choice in this.

I realized that the Warden was working with the light fae...that was a new development.

Seth must have been taken here specifically so the Warden could have access to him. So that he could hunt down the scepter.

The Warden didn't seem like a person who did anything out of the goodness of his heart, so what was he getting out of this arrangement? Gold? More artifacts for his collection?

"You will start right away, and you will be success-ful," he assured me, as if failure wasn't an option.

My arms were trembling by my side. "I don't know if I can do this. What if he sees through my lies and goes crazy on me?"

"I never said you had a choice, and I'm sure you can work it all out," he snapped. "And of course, I'm not going to make you do this without giving you some-thing in return."

I stilled, knowing there were only a few things in the world that I actually cared about. And one of them was in this room.

"If you succeed, I will give you back your power." His gaze drifted over to the shelf where my golden orb sat.

He had me. And he knew it.

With that power, I could finally take control of my life, escape Julian, and follow my own life. Freedom lay so close, and I drew my bottom lip into my mouth, gnawing on it.

Meeting the Warden's eyes, I asked the question plaguing my mind. "And if I fail?"

He huffed and ran a hand over his mouth before he reclined into his seat. "Well, Selena, if you fail, I will be adding at least ten more years to your sentence at Nightmare Penitentiary." He gave a wry smile and got to his feet, signaling the end of the conversation.

I couldn't move. I sat there completely speechless.

I'd forgotten the fact that in my life, things could always get worse.

But I would do anything to feel the call of the siren flowing through my veins once again.

Even steal secrets from a murderer.

It was time to get to work. Any chance of happiness depended on it.

It wasn't betrayal if we weren't friends.

Right?

C.R. JANE

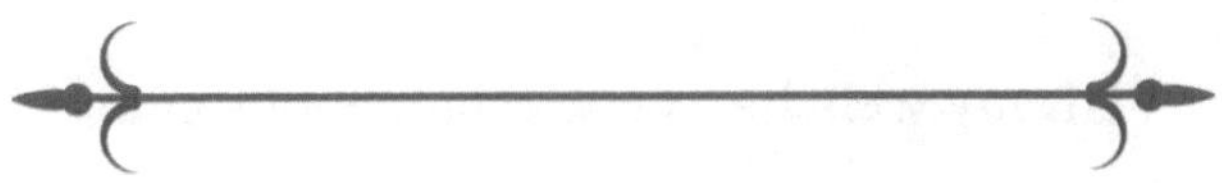

A Texas girl living in Utah now, I'm a wife, mother, lawyer, and now author. My stories have been floating around in my head for years, and it has been a relief to finally get them down on paper. I'm a huge Dallas Cowboys fan and I primarily listen to Beyonce and Taylor Swift...don't lie and say you don't too.

My love of reading started probably when I was three and with a faster than normal ability to read, I've devoured hundreds of thousands of books in my life. It only made sense that I would start to create my own worlds since I was always getting lost in others'.

I like heroines who have to grow in order to become badasses, happy endings, and swoon-worthy, devoted, (and hot) male characters. If this sounds like you, I'm pretty sure we'll be friends.

I'm so glad to have you on my team...check out the

links below for ways to hang out with me and more of my books you can read!

Join my Facebook readers' group:
www.facebook.com/groups/C.R.FatedRealm/

Visit my website: www.crjanebooks.com/

MILA YOUNG

Bestselling author, Mila Young tackles everything with the zeal and bravado of the fairytale heroes she grew up reading about. She slays monsters, real and imaginary, like there's no tomorrow. By day she rocks a keyboard as a marketing extraordinaire. At night she battles with her might pen-sword, creating fairytale retellings, and sexy ever after tales. In her spare time, she loves pretending she's a mighty warrior, walks on the beach with her dogs, cuddling up with her cats, and devouring every fantasy tale she can get her pinkies on.

Join my Facebook reader group.
www.facebook.com/groups/milayoungwicke-
dreaders

www.ingramcontent.com/pod-product-compliance
Lightning Source LLC
Chambersburg PA
CBHW020806190726
48285CB00006B/2180